A Leopard in my Bed

A LEOPARD IN MY BED

AND OTHER STORIES

Patrick Mangeni wa'Ndeda

MALLORY

Published by
Mallory Publishing,
Aylesbeare Common Business Park,
Exmouth Road,
Aylesbeare,
Devon,
EX5 2DG,
England

For a complete list of titles, visit
http://www.mallorypublishing.co.uk
e-mail: admin@mallorypublishing.co.uk

First published 2006 by Mallory Publishing
Copyright © Patrick Mangeni wa'Ndeda 2006
Cover photograph of the author
© Harriet Mangeni 2006

ISBN 1 85657 105 x

Cover design © Mallory International Limited 2006

Mallory New African Writing

An Introduction to the Series

All of us at Mallory International are delighted to have the opportunity to launch a new fiction series, incorporating innovative work from young writers in Africa, in conjunction with the British Council. *New African Writing* features unpublished works, some of it by previously unpublished authors.

Mallory International is primarily a bookseller, and most of our business is in Africa, so we have a commitment to African education and culture, and publishing gives us an opportunity both to publish new works and (through our *Classic African Writing* series) to improve the availability of past African classics which have been allowed to go out of print.

I need to record our thanks to Richard Weyers, Director of the British Council in Uganda. *New African Writing* was his idea, and he describes overleaf how it came about. I think it is the kind of initiative which shows the British Council at its best.

We are interested in developing both parts of our list, and if you know of (or have written) an important book now out of print – or if you are a new author without a publisher, please get in touch. No promises, but we will certainly have a look. Contact details are on our website, at http://www.malloryint.co.uk

Julian Hardinge
February, 2006

Foreword

It's a special kind of privilege to be able to help others realise their dreams. Publishers regularly fulfil that role and in this case the British Council too, through this happy partnership with Mallory International. *New AfricanWriting* is an attempt to bring more of the incredibly vibrant writing coming out of Africa to a wider public. It is based on a very successful programme of creative writing called *Crossing Borders*. Since 2001 nearly 200 talented young writers from Cameroon, Ghana, Kenya, Malawi, Nigeria, South Africa, Uganda and Zimbabwe have participated in this distance learning creative writing programme delivered by the British Council in collaboration with the University of Lancaster in the UK and many African partners. *Crossing Borders* began in Uganda and it is therefore only appropriate that this series should begin with some of the best new writing coming out of Uganda.

For more information about Crossing Borders please see www.crossingborders-africanwriting.org

The British Council is the United Kingdom's international organisation for educational opportunities and cultural relations. It connects people worldwide with learning opportunities and creative ideas from the UK and builds lasting relationships between the UK and other countries.

RichardWeyers
Director
British Council Uganda

Contents

A Leopard in my bed

The day was winding up. The sun, which had accomplished yet another of its chores, was descending to the other end of the world to adventure in the mysteries of the unknown. It smiled a tired ray of orange ripened by the wear and tear from the day's attendance. Through the swamps and the thickets, we were forging our way home. It was six o'clock. Unusually, we had been discharged from school an hour earlier to enable us reach our homes before night blinded earth with her bleak mask. For, in our village and those beyond, a stranger had been sighted.

It was Omwogi, the village senior bachelor, who had broken the news to the men of the village.

"Abalukhya, I do not know whether it was my eyes which deceived me," he had started.

"How do we know it was not your mandibles?" a notorious youth had retorted. Ignoring this calculated insult, which was aimed at his rather prominent jaws, Omwogi went ahead to whisper that, the previous night, as he was returning from drinking, he had sighted what looked like a gigantic animal of the cat family. In reaction, his clansmen had summarily booed him down, dismissing his fears as a drunken hallucination of a cowardly kind. Omwogi was such a coward that he could not even trust his own shadow.

The night of that day was, however, not slow in reinforcing the siren of the coward. Like thunder that bolts from a seemingly virgin sky, there had burst such a cry of the wildest kind that had numbed the chirrup of the cricket and silenced the harmonies of all other nocturnal choristers. Then it had come again and all dogs had led the way as men pursued them to a common sanctuary. The third cry had put a full stop to any remaining doubt. It was the father of horror; so terrifying that it surpassed that of the fiercest beast in Lukhya mythology. Unfinished meals and uncompleted sentences were to be continued the next day, if the stranger so willed.

In the morning, on our way to school, something moved in the grass by the roadside and we screamed, scattering like mice. Recovering from the shock we saw my dog Kilima. It crossed the path with something that looked like the ear of a goat. We turned the bend to find a host of other dogs fighting over some more animal remains and running across to the nearest homestead we were treated to a glimpse of the capabilities of our stranger. Odundo had woken up to find the scattered entrails of what had been his pregnant goat, the pudding of stomach, liver and embryo, mashed in blood, urine, dung and earth: this was surely the stranger's hand. What a way to kill! Dogs were having their fill.

Excluding the time we would spend climbing trees for fruit, being chased around by bullies and swimming in the ponds, we would take approximately about one hour from school to our homes. But the sprint of this evening, lubricated by the communal fear of an abrupt pounce, panted down the distance to less than twenty minutes.

Along the way, we would meet our male parents

either coming towards school or anxiously waiting for us with their spears. Our file steadily kept losing its count to the road junctions.

I was now alone. Rounding the last bend to enter home, I sighted my mother waiting with a Goliath of a club. Throwing the club down, she started running towards me.

"*Mama Omumbeja!*" She addressed me as Princess mother because I was one of the incarnations of her mother in-law's sister, for I was one of those named after her.

"Are you okay?" she asked, holding me by the shoulders and looking into my eyes, like she used to do, when as a child, I would return to her whimpering after a playmate had levelled a fist on the ridge of my skull. I nodded, feeling rather uneasy with the pampering.

"Who does this Headmaster of yours think he is? Is he a stranger to the ill-health that has infected this village?" She pointed her finger in the direction of the school, "Next time I meet him, he will curse the day he popped out of his mother's womb." She did this as she led me into the house, like she used to do in those early days after father would have insulted me with a slap for not scrubbing my back.

I felt tender. I realised how little interested in my life my teachers were. A clog of bitterness choked my throat. How I would have loved to golf the ribs of one of them with that Goliath of mother's club, I thought. I felt supple and a tear rolled down my cheek, reminding me of those tender days when she would lay me on her lap, removing insects from my hair and wax from my ears.

We had a quick supper, which was normally our only meal for the day, school being too far for us to return home for lunch and our parents being too poor to buy us a meal at school.

For a bath, mother could not let us go outside. She took us to the visitors' room. In turns, we stood in one basin and bathed from another.

Dragging her Goliath behind her, she saw us to our cottage. Despite the fact that our father, being a civil servant, lived away from the village, we - being men in the making - were not expected to sleep in our parent's house.

"Whoever thinks he must go out should finish it here!" mother stressed, pointing into an old metallic bucket.

"Not in that bucket!" I promised myself. "What if the stranger heard it resonating? In case of any moments of pressure, I would rather do it on the wall," a voice inside me swore. Seeing to it that we had locked the door, she bid us goodnight – *Lwamuchuli!*

The time was three in the morning when it happened. I felt something inside my bed. It was under the same raincoat I was covering myself with. At first, it was like a dream. But when I stirred from my half-sleep, I realised I was not being teased by a slumbering head on the loose. It was a reality. Without doubt, there was an animal in my bed. I was terrified to numbness. I was sweating, shaking, shivering; my body was all fire. My heart was racing. I could feel it thudding; it was splitting against my chest. I was paralysed. I tried to open my mouth but my lips fell back like a heavy lid. I cried unto God to ferment this reality into a dream, to pity the unripeness of my age and the innocence of my fate.

"If I must meet my hour at so early an age, why must it be now and in this manner too?" I muttered.

The animal which had been quiet since I woke up made a movement; a slight one and stopped. It had edged closer to me. Our combined weight on this bed, with its loose springs simply helped to gather both the animal and me in the depression, which our weight had formed in the middle of the bed.

It was a heavy animal.

It was a long one too. For it stretched from my head and down to beyond my waist. It must have entered while we were still in the main house. I was certain.

But can a real leopard have waited this long? Then it dawned on me. It must have entered through those wide ventilators.

Mother had always implored me to gag them with thorns. But, in my usual way, I had ignored her. I wished I had heeded her; even just for once! Possibly my fate would have been different now. My big head had cost me my life.

Then I felt some longish thing, glide over my thigh. The other end of it twitched; it was the tail of the animal. It was doing like all cats do before pouncing on their prey. I felt the spikes of its fur bulge out, piercing into my naked body like those of some monstrous skin scorching tropical caterpillar.

There was no time to waste. The mouse that goes on its knees just brings the cat closer. I had to wake up William. But all this was to be done with utmost care not to alert the animal.

But William was such a deep sleeper that not even death could stir him from his slumber. Thrice I called him, and thrice he changed sides, only to slump into yet a deeper snore.

I called again, louder this time. The fifth time, and to my astonishment, both William and the animal suddenly became quiet. No breathing. No motion. No nothing! It was still silence. A haunting silence of a calculating hunter and the slippery hunted. The three of us were listening to each other; waiting for each other. Then William broke the silence.

"What is it?" he asked on a note, more silent than I had ever heard him before.

"An animal," my whisper trembled back. And to my surprise, for the first time, the animal slowly and slightly edged from me and sniffed.

Silence.

"Was that you?" William asked in a more subdued tone.

"No!" I answered.

Then silence.

Then a squeak of a bed, and I realised I had sounded an alarm bell. William would not take chances. A small crunch of a hinge, then a thud outside. Then fading footsteps. William had fled. He had escaped. He had left me to die alone, to be torn to death. To be ripped by the unrelenting claws and hungry canines of a wild beast.

The animal sniffed again and immediately sprang to its feet. Then another movement; very slow this time. Then its belly over my left cheek. I realised it was now standing over me with its hind limbs to the back of my head and the fore ones to the front. I remembered Odundo's goat. My heart stopped. An eternity passed.

"Mother! Mother!" it was William's voice.

"What is it ,William?"

"An animal."

"Where?"

"In Patrick's bed."

"And where is Patrick?"

"Together!"

A squeak of a door, helter-skelter sounds. She was racing for our cottage with a torch of burning grass; like she had been waiting for the moment, with William dragging the Goliath in the security of her rear. Brandishing the torch ahead, mother was approaching like a swift.

I clenched my teeth and started counting long strands of time: countless eternities like an expectant mother. Then a harsh beam of light shot into the house. And with a long pole searching ahead of it, mother was determined to kill a leopard for the first time. Then she met its eyes. They were shining, reflecting all the light that was falling on them.

Then suddenly, without warning, and like all cats do, it sprang straight into the middle of the room and stopped as soon as it had leapt. It was now facing mother. She did not move. She just stood still, ready, waiting for it. Then it started going down, sinking on its belly but keeping its eyes in mother's face. Then it dawned on her, clear as the light of day, and she sighed. It was my dog Kilima.

On the Last day

Ouma had just completed his final year examinations. This was his last day at the University. From his room in the Northcote Hall of residence, the din of the customary Hall drums filled the air. A barrage of *verbal missiles,* as the students commonly referred to the trading of inter-hall insults, was being launched towards the neighbouring Nkrumah Hall. Despite belonging to a most militant student hall of residence whose conduct was as violent as it was infectious; this aspect of hall culture had never been to his fancy. He resented the often immature and violent conduct of university students in the so-called culture of protecting and advancing 'hall sovereignty'. He had strongly despised the inter-hall violence that was a likely aftermath of a football match between his hall and their professed archrivals of Lumumba Hall. He couldn't forget the time during his first year when Mukiibi, his roommate, ended up in hospital after a fight in which stones were hurled. On this particular day, a student had molested the Vice-Chancellor of the University. This kind of behaviour could not be excused in the name of 'Hall culture' and from then on he always walked away when he heard the sound of drums.

Ouma sighed. The noise outside was approaching like a storm. He fingered his keys uneasily, picked them up, pushed them into his jacket pocket and moved to his window. His final paper gave him a feeling of having crossed the line. He did not feel so much a part of student life any more. He was waiting for the next day to go back home and help his parents on the farm. He planned also to do some part-time teaching at Lumino High, the secondary school near his home, as he waited for the results to be announced. It would be good practice for him before starting his teaching career, Ouma thought, smiling to himself.

Ouma had consistently received A's in the first two years of University where he was doing Literature in English and Music. The Vice-chancellor had officially acknowledged him as the best performing student. With a grade point average of 4.8, Ouma was heading for a first class degree. He had been earmarked for staff recruitment and the Dean of the Faculty had encouraged him to work harder.

"You have a very bright future ahead, Ouma Joseph. If you keep up that performance, we are going to sponsor you for your Masters. Do not lose your focus." The examinations had been easy and he knew where he was headed. 'Books first everything else later' he would intone before humming to himself.

So as he stood in the now empty yard, he could hear the din from the drums go up the Main Hall towards the football pitch. He felt like taking a walk. To where? He did not know. But he just wanted to walk to somewhere.

Although the evening haunted him with a desire to free himself of the now boring routine of student life, he was undecided where to stroll. All he felt was a growing urge to be free.

As he trudged towards the Main Hall, the air was calmer. The sun was just setting and the Main Hall tower stood out prominently like Kim II Sung's monument of 'Juche'. A calm easterly breeze whistled through the giant jacarandas of the Library Park and as they turned, a sweet fragrance from the freshly mown grass brought the freshness of the country air. In the nearby St. Francis Chapel, the Kampala Singers performance of Handel's *Messiah* was irresistible. The melody was that of the seraphs and cherubs at a celestial dinner. There were about five people in the audience. Two of them stooping professors of Mathematics, the Vice Chancellor who held his head high as if he was posing for press cameras, the Archbishop whose mind was in 'minor key' and a middle aged lady who listened with a plastic smile. But no sooner had he listened to one movement than he started feeling congested; the soles of his feet itching. He turned uncomfortably on the pew like a laying hen. What did he want? Where did he want to go? He knew no answer. But at least he knew what he felt. He just felt out of place. Rather than force himself to stay, he got up and followed his feet.

The urge, somehow, led him to the gates of Complex Hall; fondly called 'crocodile land' because residents were referred to as crocodiles. Now he could call on one of his friends and chat about how the exams were and their prospects in their field of study. As he was contemplating which of his friends he should visit, a female voice came,

"Hallo, mature!" It sounded familiar.

"Hallo, pre-mature!" he sighed back inquisitively,

trying to locate in his mind whom it was.

"What *crocodile* has stolen your heart?" she approached. It was Jane. A third year student of Statistics.

"It's her skin I seek," he quipped, turning to her. They faced each other awkwardly. "It is a long time, Jane!" he smiled back instinctively saying what crossed his lips. "I heard you changed rooms."

"Since when?" she dared him with a theatrical frown on her face.

"Since Jesus was at school," he answered and they laughed as he played it off safe and light.

At 22, Jane was a mortal harvest. Ouma looked at her admiringly and thought the creator had spent his time well. She had eyes of a calf. She was tall, she was black and she walked like a deer. She knew she had eyes and she used those eyes well. Ouma often said nature had been lavish with her.

His heart thumped, and he blushed. Realising she had noticed it, he scratched his chin and tried to look as though he was lost in Socratic thought. Her feminine sensibilities stepped in immediately to restore him.

"Eh, why not join me in seeing off this cake?" she smiled, pointing to the cake she was carrying. "I just bought it in the canteen."

Visiting Jane, he decided, would not be a bad way to pass the evening, he thought, licking the fringes of his sprouting moustache.

Jane was also a very gifted student; she loved her books - just as much as she loved kissing, he seemed to remember. He smiled a sigh of surrender, and followed her up the stairs.

Ouma looked at her legs as she went ahead of him. They looked more beautiful with each step she made. He liked their shape, he liked their elegance, he liked their fullness and he liked the soft baby skin. He was now staring into them. She said something to him but he did not hear. He was just staring at her legs as they climbed. Climbing with them. Climbing in them. There was now this feeling that was beginning to tempt him downward; to dip his tongue into the dimples of those legs. Then he bumped into something; it was her back. He looked up and noticed that she had stopped. She turned to smile at him, stepped aside and pointed ahead for him to lead the way.

Ouma had first met Jane in their first year at University when they had both attended an instrumental of Bach's "Jesu, joy of man's desiring" performed by the department of Music, Dance and Drama of Makerere University. On that day, the hall had been packed to capacity like a church on Christmas Day, not out of any classical taste on the part of the predominantly student audience but more because of a break dance show that would begin soon after. Ouma, who amidst the pushing and squeezing had secured himself a seat, was awakened to a voice asking to share with him. He had ignored it, but when it persisted, he looked up into a lady's eyes and what he saw broke something inside him. Throughout the performance, and to this day, all he remembered of the performance was the glow in her eyes and the warm feeling of her hip on his side. From that time on they became friends and saw each other often.

And just when they were beginning not to care about what the world around them was saying, after one of Jane's visits to his room, Mukiibi, his roommate, had fallen in love with her. He had spent a week describing two things; her eyes and legs and how deep they had condemned his heart to a sentence he must serve. He said he would just die and die again and again if Ouma did not honourably step down, in solidarity. "I will give you anything for that girl," he moaned. Ouma knew there would be no peace if he did not relent. Besides, his growing involvement with Jane in the past few weeks had cost him lower grades on two assignments. So Ouma, to Jane's puzzlement, had given this relationship a second thought and then retreated to the library.

Mukiibi made his move and soon, he and Jane were to be seen side by side; at the Guild canteen and beyond the gates of Makerere. "A man can now die!" Mukiibi had said one afternoon after having woken beside her that morning. Ouma hadn't known what was to happen - how could he? But now he couldn't think of those words without a chill running through him. He missed Mukiibi. He wondered if Jane did too.

Staring into his half-empty cup of coffee, Ouma remembered that conversation with Mukiibi vividly as he turned the last leaf of Jane's photo album, which he had seen more than once before but only took from her out of politeness. He noticed that something was missing in it; Mukiibi's photographs. There had always been one on the first and last leaves of the album. Turning towards her pillow, he noticed that the photo of him that had always been by bedside was also missing.

Their eyes met and Jane looked away with a mixture of pain and something like guilt. He sighed, fumbling with the cup of coffee remnants in his hands. Remorsefully, Ouma recalled the scene of Mukiibi's premature death in that accident; a pudding of bone, flesh and blood smeared on the tarmac by a trailer that had failed to swerve.

For a long time after this grotesque spectacle, Ouma could not imagine that he would ever eat meat or touch liver again. A policeman who had extracted Mukiibi's identity card from the mass of flesh and bone had called the University and soon the Hall warden had picked up Ouma and their Hall chairman to accompany him to the scene to help in identification.

He grimaced thoughtfully as he put aside the album and sipped cold coffee absentmindedly. Jane sighed. A silence whose hollowness defied filling, descended in between them. Ouma's mind got bogged on the subject of this silence. He turned like he had heard something ominous. He could hear in the corridors, heavy shoes approaching at a measured pace. They sounded distant but familiar. Ouma could not remember whose they were. But they sounded familiar. The footsteps became more cautious and softer as they approached. The silence was magnified by the ghostly sensation that surrounded their haunting grotesqueness. Ouma felt taut. The feet came close to the door and stopped. Jane who had been watching Ouma closely now looked confused. He looked up and their eyes met. Ouma looked to the latch of the door. Jane too looked at the latch, wondering. It did not turn. "Ouma, what is the matter?" she asked. But he did not hear. He was just staring at the door. He then heard the footsteps. They were going away, back towards where they had come from. Back down stairs. "Who was that?" he asked quietly. "Who?"

His hand reached for his coffee. It was now cold, really cold. He lifted it to his lips, paused and put it back slowly, without drinking from it. He swallowed a dry throat and looked at her. She was still staring at him with a blankness that seeped into him, through him, beyond him, to that infinity that had come in the silence and claimed it. She sighed and got up. There were tears that shone like beads of silver in her eyes. She turned towards the wardrobe, opened it quietly, her back taut with uneasiness. Her hand went up higher on the cross-bar and took a towel towards her face.

She turned around with a shallow smile. That put some life back into this room that had suddenly chilled and haunted them. She signalled for him to shift his chair from the window side to allow her to clear the cups. Although he knew that it was not necessary for him to shift to enable her to remove a cup and a teapot, he got the message in her aching stare; he was in the same place and seat that Mukiibi used to occupy.

A female voice screamed outside demanding an explanation as to why someone had again used her meal card to claim her food. She was threatening to call a press conference if the offender did not give a public apology.

Jane and Ouma burst into snotty laughter easing the tension. She giggled more and laughed throwing her neck back and he liked the cascades that rippled its length. Ouma though, still had no words and they fell quiet again.

He could not bear this any longer. He must get out of here and sprang to his feet. He was leaving.

"What is the matter?" she asked curtly.

"Just stretching my lousy feet." he answered and immediately wondered why he had said such a thing. Why in the first place had he not just stated his mind? The kind of feeling he had for Jane when they first met. This feeling was beginning to stir him again. It was beginning to cloud his mind. Deep inside him there was something he was sensing, something like the fear of the probable truth began to cloud his mind. He was in no mood to cope with disappointment. He feared losing her. Then sheepishly smiling, he heard himself inviting her for a beer at the Guild Canteen. He bit his lower lip, berating himself. Wanting to escape from the room too, she promptly accepted and with a deep sigh they walked to the door.

One year on, Mukiibi's death still haunted him. Could he have dived into the trailer's path, to heal himself of a certain, slow and painful death? He wondered, popping the second bottle of Nile Special. Mukiibi had suffered from recurrent fever for a protracted time. And he had lost weight considerably. His eyes stuck out of his head like demonstration ball bearings and the skin on his torso hung like a shirt on a hanger. Sores had filled his mouth and his bowels moved when he was not aware. As his roommate, Ouma had seen the close up deterioration of his friend's health, he waited for him to confide on him. But it never happened. The trailer had claimed his friend and confidant, first.

After his burial, the whole of Northcote Hall argued over whether he had killed many or many had eventually killed him. They would count on their hands until they ran short of fingers. But every time they counted, Jane was among them; claiming the first or the second finger.

"When did your affair with Mukiibi stop?"

"Why?" She jolted a bit, pushing her beer back.

"Ah… I was simply asking." They looked away from each other in the semi-darkness.

"About one…. I mean two years ago. Why?" she looked him in the face.

"Nothing much," he shrugged his shoulders. Ouma smiled an insecure and shallow smile into this darkness between them.

"Ouma, are you fearing me because you think that he could have committed suicide?"

"No … I was just wondering."

"You do not have to worry yourself if you do not feel comfortable with me." She paused. "We had broken up and I do not want to go into that now."

She remembered the day she argued with another woman over Mukiibi. They were entering a restaurant in Wandegeya township when a lanky lady barely plastered in a swimsuit grabbed Mukibi by the fly of his trousers and demanded her money. When a blinking Mukiibi denied any knowledge of her, the woman yelled so loudly that she quickly attracted a sizeable crowd. She accused him of having slept with her on credit and then defaulting on payment. At first Jane, like many around, did not believe until she mentioned his name, Hall of Residence and room number and named the four fingernail scars across his buttocks. Jane had burst into tears, pulled out a five hundred shilling note and cast it to the woman.

That night she had wept. Her chest got so wet, she had to spread her nightdress on the drying line. She was heavy with embarrassment. She was hurting. She had always suspected him to be reckless but not to this extent. That is why she had insisted on condoms from the start, except for one day when she had woken up to find herself in his bed, naked and damp. Mukiibi was not there. When he returned to find her in tears and confused, he explained that they had returned from the Hall re-union party and that she was drunk and would not hear of keeping their clothes on. He had borrowed condoms from the neighbouring room, he said and had disposed of the used condoms that morning while she was asleep. She did not know whether to believe him or not.

But after the incident, she did not want to hear about him. His death had worried her and made her sad too. Once, a friend whom she was to act as bridesmaid for asked Jane to accompany her to an AIDS information centre. She tried to persuade Jane to test as well. But Jane had declined explaining that she, unlike the friend who was doing it for a pre-marital requirement, was under no such obligation. She was not prepared for it. She said she would concentrate on her books, make new friends and live her life. So Jane had put the past behind her. She was happy with it that way. She did not want the ghost of Mukiibi to haunt her. She wanted just to enjoy her life.

She sipped her beer and smiled at Ouma meekly.

Ouma smiled blankly back. He was lost in thought. He recollected seeing them in intimate company three months before Mukiibi's death, at night against the back wall of St. Augustine's Chapel. Mukiibi's white cap was unmistakable. Curiosity had denied Ouma breakfast and led him to the spot, the following morning, where he counted a cluster of partially fresh condoms. That week, he thought the Chaplain was right in his circular to the University community and its visitors to show fear of God and respect the sanctity of holy grounds. Is she being honest? Could she be censoring truth in self-interest? May be she knows she has IT as word has it. But she doesn't look like she has it … but could Jane lie to me… when it involves my life… Can such beauty be void of heart as to risk another's life…. He gulped another mouthful. Some of it went the wrong way and he fought hard against choking. He fought it and cleared his voice. His eyes watered slightly…is she meddling with the truth as a shield against stigmatisation? Questions and questions ploughed his mind. He looked at her searchingly as she rolled her eyes. Desire surged through him. The temptation to have her was growing by the minute. Jane was too beautiful. Jane was too beautiful to be false, he swore. Ouma swallowed nearly half a bottle of beer and stared ahead as if one conjuring courage, feeling the yeast warming up his skull, certain lightness in his head as if he was spinning around in the game of *dedededede kalira munamwenge.*

"Is anything the matter? You look distant!" she asked straining to focus on his face in the low light.

"I was thinking what beautiful eyes you have!" he whispered, a certain approaching resignation lining his voice. She complemented him with a look through the eyelashes; He was literally feeling her in his loins, his underside churning with a lemonish tingling sensation. It had been brewing over time. The predilection to have her gained another scale. 'The only way of getting rid of a temptation is by yielding to it'- the adage crossed his heart and loosened his fancies.

She popped her fifth beer. The sound pronounced another period of stalemate.

The proverb of a boat that capsizes as it is about to anchor crossed his mind and he sighed.

Was Jane worth the risk? Had he not spent his three years of study usefully, faithfully and safely? Why the hurry? What for? Yes he could wait for his day, his girl…. But is there any difference between these girls anyway? Right now the so-called Miss right could be giving some rascal *a lift.*

He opened his third bottle.

If I am asking myself all these questions am I not trying to be wiser than fate? He recalled that he had nearly lost his life three times. He had once shared a blanket with a black mamba; when still a boy and in the mango season, he had fallen off a branch and slumped between chiselled tree stumps and he'd unknowingly eaten poisoned fish that his grandmother had set to trap house mice … I could not have survived this by sheer chance, he thought God must have been protecting me for a purpose, some wonderful plan for me… can He then be as godless as to lure or watch me die … Can a real God have the heart to watch the only son of a widowed mother; my mother, eaten by a beauty of death? Can He, when He commands the power for all to cease, turn and progress at His will. A true parent like God can have no hand in that… He Himself must have led me to Jane this evening…the Lord always works in strange ways. Positive thoughts progressively crowded his mind.

She gave him an inviting smile and he felt its warmth stir his heart. …. She cannot have it…

He gulped another mouthful of beer.

Well, even if she did, where is the guarantee that I would contract it… Yes I would go about it the slow and smooth way, that way I would avoid bruising myself, maximise pleasure and avoid being infected with AIDS…. He swallowed a dry throat and paused in his thought. But even if I got it, would I be the first or last? … Well, if my time has come then it has come… I could even live with it for ten or more years… hasn't it been said that some people have been HIV positive for over ten years without breaking down? And in ten years time a cure should have been found. Or I could even eventually get used to it and join those who are living positively with AIDS. Everything has its positive side. He felt more encouraged.

A ray of light licked her chest, revealing her nipples. He was gnawed with the urge to squeeze them, to suck them … His lips twitched, leaking out the finer bits of his emotion. He slipped his right hand under the table and touched her bare thigh and she lowered her head and paused as if she was listening to him. He snaked the hand up the thigh. She held his hand, gently. "Ouma, it's not safe." She mumbled with alluring resistance. He started getting strong. Charging in cascades of desire.

Like most women, she does not want to take the initiative… he thought, his breath rising in a crescendo, a relentless ghost stalking the night of his fate. He groped his hand under the table, held hers and pressed it with the tender hardness of lovers taking advantage of a sudden blackout.

"It is not safe, Ouma!" she said, lowering her hand under the table and stroking his hairy arms. He felt her tremble in her fingers, her eyelids heavy with fruit; she was finished.

"Jane, I need you like I will never need again."

"Ouma, please, let's not lose control," she barely whispered with helpless warmth.

"I am in full control," he whispered back as their feet fell towards Northcote Hall.

"Ouma, do you have protection to wear," she mumbled, leaning on his torso.

"Relax. I will take care of us," he cooed, his spirits buoying, her warmth lining his side. Surely, if Jane had it, what would the symptoms still be waiting for… at least a cough… a pimple, even just on the nose… he hooked his fingers into the warmth of her fleshy hips. Can death be so warm? Besides, Mukiibi never had sex without condoms… so Jane cannot have got it. He paused with a shadow of hesitation… what of an odd day… but most times Mukiibi brought women when he was too drunk to for abrasive sex. This should have eliminated the risk of infection for Jane. He swallowed warm saliva. But what of an odd day? There must be a day for things to go wrong… that is when Mukiibi could be wearing a condom. Ouma's spirits touched the stars.

"Jane, when … when … could I ask something?"

"Mh?"

"Have you always … I mean, used condoms … before?"

"Are you asking if … if I mind them?" He nodded.

"They are safer."

He looked into her face and their eyes locked.

Save for the heavy breathing, a silence covered their lazy feet as they felt their way past the statue of Kwame Nkrumah in the quadrangle of Nkrumah Hall. But what could be worrying her? Why is she so quiet? He wondered. The problem with some of us Africans is that we are either busy being suspicious or superstitious. Let the departed nurse their own spirits!

In the corridors of the Hall, a lone voice saluted him, declaring him a 'Field Marshal' for daring the uncertainties of combat in this dangerous era.

He banged back the door with his foot, kicked off the

shoes in splitting directions as his hands reached for the drawer of his reading table. He fished out his roommate's spectacles case and flipped out two *protector* condoms. The mathematics was simple; the more condoms applied at a go the less the risk of infection.

Even if a bomb had gone off behind him, Ouma would not have flinched. Even if the world had ended, Ouma would have witnessed it second hand. He was sailing on rejuvenated waves of pleasure, pleasure in arrears. How have I been living without this? Sex in a condom had always been equated to sucking a sweet with the wrappings on. But with Jane the sweet was covering the wrapping.

Uncoiling he rolled over and pulled up the pillow to his head. He inhaled the air. The smell of sex reminded him of fresh fish. He turned his head, winked at Jane and, with a mellow smile, looked down his naked body as if to thank a part of himself. He stopped and sat up suddenly. "Oh, mama ... mama ...!" he screamed like a man with a soldier termite on the tip of his manhood.

"What is it, Ouma?" Jane leapt up, the raffled sheets peeling off her naked body. A crumpled condom fell on the floor. Jane shook the sheets desperately as if she had lost something. Then turned to Ouma who was on his knees perched on the pillow-sobbing, "But I had put on two! But I had put on...." A broken condom hopelessly hung to his manhood, like a T-shirt.

Greeting relatives

"Have you heard?" Father asked.

William lowered his head and answered, "Yes, Father."

"Now repeat what I said."

"Aunt Sarah, this is the fish that father promised you…"

Father picked William's head with a knuckle and his stammer tapered off.

"Five fish, my son. You saw me counting. Five fish!" our other mother emphasised as she did the last flap of the newspaper, rolling the parcel, placing it in the basket and looping it across William's shoulder. "Now say it as your father has told you."

"Aunt Sarah, this is the supper that father promised you. Inside this basket there is five fish. He sends you greetings and goodbye." And William sighed.

"Cross the road from the usual point, at the palm nut tree and nowhere else. There are too many madmen peddling down the slope." Our other mother said.

"Where is Patrick?" Father turned to where my voice answered his call. "Escort your brother. Cross the road at the usual place carefully and you move straight to-?" he left me to fill in as usual.

"Sarah's place —"

And turning to William "To where?"

"Sarah's place," he replied, a little higher than Father's voice.

"And what else should a good child always remember?" our other mother stressed.

"You should never wait to eat what you have been given to take to somebody," William replied, fastening the basket.

"Or else?" she continued appearing not amused by the lightness with which William had answered.

"*Khajwinjwini* the bird will come and burn your household," I said, hopping ahead of William.

"Do not let anybody trick you to let him peep into that basket. And remember I want you here before it's dark." Father said, picking his night gear in preparation for the night shift.

"My children hurry up. Mugusita was released yesterday," our other mother said.

That was the worst thing a mother could tell another woman's child at that time. It was like someone leaving you in the dark with the body of a stranger. Mugusita, standing at seven feet plus, was the most chilling inmate in the barracks. It was said he had strangled his lover and her lover in one swoop. But that's not what terrified people most. It was the extra finger and toe he had on each of his limbs. At the count of twenty-four his limbs gave him a crabby monstrous spread, each of them appearing like some searching projectile. I always had this thought that if he dispatched his full capacity; one might escape some but all of them. Often when I walked from Camp Swahili, a near by suburb where we would be sent to buy groceries, I sprinted across that stretch, where the bodies of his victims were found, imagining an octopus of limbs fanning out for some little prey.

On crossing the fence that separated the Prisons barracks from the freer world, William was the first to notice that the Soroti-Moroto road was not busy at the time, but I reminded William that mother had advised us against crossing the road from any other spot apart from the one ahead. But it seemed like William had other ideas. There were many people on either side of the road, like safari ants that have been disrupted. Most of these were Prison staff that had returned from Lake Kyoga where the Prison's truck occasionally went to collect cheaper fish. They were now fanning out. Some like Okadapau were waiting for transport to Camp Swahili to drink or meet the mothers of their other children.

Nobody seemed to notice our disagreement with William. Then within the time it takes a chicken to pick an ant a voice of a woman pierced the air.

A bicycle had missed William by a finger's length. The fish split out of the basket like silver fireworks. I skidded on the murram to the left wresting one of the fish from the hands of Okadapau's son. I heard laughter and handclaps. "Sergeant's son is a real commando!" a male voice commended.

Okadapau's son slithered under the fence and disappeared just like he had appeared when the fish got air bound from the basket. I turned and looked across and I saw William, his back to me.

"Why did you also cross when father warned us –?"

"I can't see one of the fish," he said combing the bush with his nails, like someone forking through Rastafarian hair.

I hopped a step and jumped over. William was now looking over a ditch next to the East African flying school fence. I went towards him but he stopped next to a culvert and turned. "Patrick. Look!" I edged closer and I saw the thing he was pointing at. It was some animal. The fur on its back was clumped in tufts like the wet feathers of a chicken.

"William, let me get a stone," I said my eyes fixed on it as I stepped a foot back.

"Don't!" he hushed me, "You never know what it actually is."

I looked at William. We turned our eyes to it in rehearsed motion and then, William moved a step back. And I made two quick ones, getting to his side.

"Don't disturb it. It could cross the road with the fish and father sees it." William gently tapped me behind him.

As we walked trying to fix back the other fish in the basket, I asked William if he had ever seen that particular one and he licked his finger swiped it over his throat and swore that it was his first time to see it. It was my first time too, I swore imitating the motions of his finger.

"Look!" William pointed lowering his body closer to the ground.

"What is it?" I fell one head lower than him, a blade of grass licking my nose.

"Look at who is coming."

39

"You see now, I told you we should not cross the road, but-," I said feeling a film of tears dancing in my eyes.

"Shh…" William ran his finger across the lips and I went silent. And he hauled me across the road.

Mrs. Akadapao was a friend of our other mother. But that was not the problem or even that she was going to hot-comb our other mother's hair that evening. It is that Mrs. Akadapao was more likely to talk everything she thought of than think of what she talked of. And she telling father that we had crossed the road elsewhere would put our ears at risk. Father had always promised to remove somebody's ear one day.

"Look!" William stopped again, pointing.

"It's the one that we saw in the ditch, I swear!" My heart was sounding like a mallet.

"The other one had a brown patch, here on his forehead," William craned his head as if to ascertain without arousing its attention.

"It was grey," I disagreed.

"But…you could be right," he peered. "It now wants to look like the other one," he said taking a foot back.

"It is the one, William, I swear!"

"Patrick," he paused and took in a breath of air.

"William—" I waited anxiously.

"I think it is a ghost."

"Ghost! Do ghosts eat fish?"

William did not answer but he lifted the basket higher into his armpits and clutched it to his side like a G-cramp.

"Who does it resemble?" I turned to William running out of breath.

"Possibly Mugusita's wife or her lover…they say her shadow walks along this road coming from Camp Swahili.

"Going where?" I was more worried than interested in the answer. But William's attention was now back to it.

It looked at us, raised its nose and mapped the air in a slow spinning motion.

"They say she comes along this road on her way to that mortuary where they kept her body," he said, hardly audible.

"And what does she say when she reaches…the… when she reaches the mortuary?"

"Nothing. But she can come in form of a cat, a woman without a bra or even a mango by the roadside," William answered more or less unconsciously.

"And also as a dog?" I asked looking at it.

"I have seen dogs in the barracks but I have never seen that one." The dog stopped and looked at us.

"She has heard us." I tapped William.

It moved its nose like someone with fits and then turned suddenly, its nose hoisted, and trotted towards the other side of the mortuary.

William tugged at my hand and we hastened.

The horizon was fading in the distance and under the retreating light; a streak of lightening electrocuted the sky. A palm tree ahead hissed as a breeze raffled its leaves arm-twisting its branches. The wind continued humming its way into the darkening canopy over the mortuary. Under the darkening shades, a thread of smoke rose filtering into the air. Below an ember glowed before another spurt of smoke rose losing its line in the distance. It was Bokilo the Mortuary attendant spread under the leaves with the confidence of a rainmaker, as he continued to puff his cigarette. Father had told us that those he found when he came to work in Soroti said they had found Bokilo working at the mortuary and that he smoked all the time to keep his nose fresh.

"William, but why doesn't he close the door to that place?"

"The bodies need fresh air," William said, narrowing his nose.

"But the smell —"

"Do not spit. If you do the spirits of the dead will haunt you and you will spit for the rest of your life," William's face was frozen as he said this. So I cupped my lips like a goat winding its rear after the last droppings.

"Don't cover your nose," William warned. "If Bokilo sees you, he will drag you in there and lock you up with those people."

True, I had heard about that. And also that all women he proposed to had refused him and that he was now befriending young dead women. That those who said bad things about him he would remind them, saying, "Wait, I will get you when you are referred to my office, then you will see who is boss." It was actually said that once he punished the corpse of a man who had insulted him,

42

while still walking this earth. That Bokilo didn't care if he was actually one of the *Mafutamingi* tycoons or the remains of such a one. That he put the fellow's body on the floor, another body opposite it, as bodies were usually arranged, then another pair across but over them, and then he proceeded to build a pyramid, dovetailing limbs and creating a jigsaw. That it was only the roof, which interrupted him. So anybody who was alive or had a relative living in Soroti knew how important it was to be nice to Bokilo, otherwise when the time came for one to claim their own from his 'office' he could send you in there to sort out who might be yours from the rest.

As I followed William who had somewhat quickly skipped across to avoid Bokilo's line of sight, I could not run for fear of spilling my mouth; I was choking with the bowl of saliva. I stopped as William signalled me to. He was keeping his eye on Bokilo from behind a coconut tree where he was hiding. He peered in the direction of the mortuary, raised his hand a little in a hold-on motion, lowered it in get-down move and then did a 'get-on-your-mark-hurry-across' sign. But I hesitated and squatted instead. He knew why. I did not like the spot he was standing crouching his basket.

I preferred to continue and link through the post office. I did not like that spot for I could still see the body, I once saw there, spreading over the length of the stretcher, the feet peeping out of the thready hospital blanket and spilling over. I could still see the body bouncing it's weight from this side to the other like the hump of a mighty bull, its cold masculine feet clearing the way like wipers on a windscreen. I could still see the four men with cold foreheads staggering on their heels making their way to the mortuary. That was the first dead body I saw. It was right where William was now standing. Then, it was on its way to the mortuary behind me.

"You! What do you want from here?" a drowsy voice came from behind me. I spun around to catch Bokilo springing to his feet and looping forward like a cat at a circus. His lanky frame danced a little before picking something. It could have been a stone. I did not wait. I ran across to William, naturally spilling the bowl in my mouth. William fidgeted to stuff me behind him, and I heard the basket and its contents fall.

"I know what you want from here but let me tell you my friend, you will not get even a finger," and, saying so, he spat on the stone, or whatever he had picked, hopped one step back, angled backward to a javelin pose and with a forward thrust released what he was holding. It went whistling in the air and caused a sound the other end. The bush moved like there was a short thick wind ruffling through it and at the end of it a dog appeared. It looked at us, sniffed with its nose hoisted, hesitated and crossed the road.

"It is following us, Patrick."

"Is it Mugusita's wife?"

William did not answer. He bent and uprooted some grass from the roadside and using air from his lungs he dusted the fish of the sand and gravels embedded in the scales. Using his finger to fork the soil out of the fish's mouth was taking long, so he got hold of my hand and changed direction. "Let's run, the sun should set when we have passed Pioneer school," he said trying to haul me along.

"No, I do not want to pass by the church," and I spread my feet like a mangrove tree.

"But Bishop Maraka lies inside and not on top of his grave." William did this as he uprooted and plucked me along, I tried to fork my feet into the ground this time like some disagreeing goat but William would not take any more of me. He grabbed me by the waist and hauled me along in a time-up manner, the same style my father did with some repeated offenders.

It was not the fear of seeing Maraka but the memories and nightmares the grave conjured that made me avoid that path often. I had never seen the face of a dead person until Bishop Maraka died and all pupils of Soroti Primary School were marched for the funeral service. I got my place among the first children. That face was dead, dead and cold. But most memorable of all was the cotton padding so generously applied in the nose and in the ears that it seemed as if they had run short of it. I thought I would never eat meat again. At school children talked of how the ghost of the bishop would come demanding that they free the body from church and take him home for a real burial. Every time I passed the church I sensed as if I was about to hear him. But this was not William's problem. But suddenly he stopped pulling me and let go off my hand, creating an imbalance that left me sprawled on the murram. The impact went up my small back. It was a miracle that I did not cry. William had stopped.

"Patrick!"

"Don't call my name. The ghost could hear and imitate you." I protested.

I don't think he even heard me as I rose to my feet looking towards his shy finger, "Look! They have come back."

In front of us with incomplete limbs stretched into the road, two lepers sat each with a tin container beside them. Another six or seven were warming themselves by a sprawling shelter of rusted iron. One of them tried to blow a fire that they had lit using what looked like a newspaper but his breath blew away the paper and the flickering flame died in the distance. Dark ash floated back dissolving in the wet ground. That house with three walls was said to be the center for lepers in Teso.

"Have the others gone to town to beg?" I wondered.

"Today is not a Friday. Muslims help beggars on Friday." William paused, looked at those by the road and continued. "Children at school said a truck came last week and people with guns and gloves helped the them climb on the tipper. They were told that Amin had found a home for all lepers in Uganda where they can be helped.

"In Kampala?"

"But that when the truck reached Awoja the tipper poured them in the lake," William continued.

"And they died?"

"That the tipper made three trips,"William continued lankly, his eyes fixed ahead. There was silence. One of the lepers with brown copper coloured hair bent to the left as if wanting to say something to the one next to him and then retreated to his former posture. He then raised a studded limb and scratched his brown and scanty copper hair.

"That dog had a brown patch, could it be a ghost of one of the lepers?" I asked.

"They can appear in many forms. They could even turn themselves into a coin by the roadside. Or they blow through the wind." We looked at each other as if on impulse and changed to a path through the medical staff quarters. I was now trotting behind William like some hunter's dog on a fruitful return journey.

When we reached the living quarters of the medical staff it was like pushing your head above the water from the bed of the ocean. We were close to a home of somebody we knew, a medical Assistant and a tribesman who was later to become a relative by marriage. We were now left with two roads to cross before reaching the nurses' quarters where Sarah lived. The medical assistant's door was open and William turned right.

"Eh, eh, this way, Sarah's home is this way," I called him, pointing to the left.

"But don't you know that it is bad manners to pass the home of people you know and you don't branch to greet them?" he said, in a scolding tone. And before I could get time to give whatever kind of response, I heard something sniff behind me and I leapt ahead of William and entered the relative's sitting room first.

"They are sons of Joseph. Don't you know the one in Prisons?" the one who welcomed us said, entering the kitchen and crossing to the sink.

"And your name again?" the one, who had asked, asked again.

"You mean you do not know Patrick?" another answered entering from the kitchen.

"I thought that one was Kaloli," the one with a raw mango said.

"Kaloli is this one," pointing at William, the one seated at in the left hand corner next to the water pot corrected the other.

"I am William," William protested before smiling at the one who had not yet said a word.

"O yah, I had forgotten, you see they resemble like fish," he said drawing water from the pot and gurgling it down.

"Kaloli is the second born," the other one tried to emphasise, picking a morsel of bread from a cold plate. He missed a speck and licked his finger.

"No, I am the second born." William said with emphasis.

"O, yes. William is the one who follows the first born?"The maid who sounded to be working at something in the kitchen clarified.

"And Kaloli follows me," I put in with a smile.

"Exactly!" said the one in a jumper, entering the bedroom.

"And father said we should hurry" I told the older of them.

"And greet him and Mummy and thank him very much for our message," he said and the maid appeared flipping the basket back to William.

The one with the jumper escorted us to the gate and closed it behind us. We stood there. The aroma of boiling fish filtered in from the direction of the house. I was facing the lepers' home. William with an empty basket was staring through teary eyes in the approaching night looking beyond the invisible skyline, staring over the light at the sentinel where father was keeping watch.

The Chimp of Chester: a memoir

Day Three: (Evening)

I turned and looked through the window. Outside, the terrain spread out with the smoothness of the plains of Teso in Eastern Uganda. Myriad of blue and galaxies of red canvassed a canopy of Christmas trees glimmering on every piece of this ground. The Mivule lights rose glowing in the bosom of the sky and fluorescent acacias flowered alloys of white and yellow in this plateau of Savannah lightlands. An arm away from the road, through the windows and into the increasingly celestial distance, it looked like a festival of fireworks, an indelible harmony choreographed on the English sky. These were enchanting angelic eyes suspended from every point of heaven, keeping vigil over this now beautiful land of the world's greatest Queen mothers.

In the distance ahead, a giant chimney gave the land a likeness of a ship docking on the Cape of Good Hope, rinsing the bowels of England, soaking her refuse into the umbra of the night. The warmth of the night was overwhelming. It spilled the heart over and I turned to her. My tongue was itching. I opened my mouth but the lips moved late, disagreed and settled without a word.

The *National Express* was now sailing like a wave. The feeling of the road was the even surface of the sea on a calm moonlit evening. It was just the cool flow of the engine and smooth gears as the coach sailed from Chester to Leeds.

My lips were really itching now. And as I turned to

her, she turned her head away sharply like a man who had caught a small glimpse of the nakedness of his mother in-law. I noticed that from the angle of her neck she was keeping an eye on me. She had been keeping an eye on me. Her heart was icy. You could feel it on her face. Instead of opening my mouth to talk, I found myself turning to a leaning position against the body of the bus (window). I then noticed that she was following my movements through the reflection in her window. Then it became clear that she had noticed that I had noticed this. A feeling mingled her face and she angled away from the window.

But I still went ahead. "Don't you think it is very beautiful – ?" and then I stopped because she had turned like a snake whose tail had been stepped on. The woman looked at me. It was a deep look; a deep look from deep down her heart. Her torso became taut, angling out like a bottom that had sensed the approaching labour of bad wind. Then her breathing had increased and shook her chest like she had an evil spirit. Then she said, "Excuse me!" Her clarity was of one paid to stress a point to a person with hearing impairment. Doing this, she rose with the motif of a professional choreographer, gathered her bags in one swipe like one divorced at short notice and she moved away. She did not look back. Laban the dance master would notate the movement simply as "Fuck off!" She moved three seats away from me and sat, her head conspicuously lined forward with the stiffness of mean legs.

Day One: Morning

At the Parkingstone Library, I called a cab. A voice on the phone hesitated before asking me whether I was the one going or someone else. Time was on my heels and I remember saying something. The cab came. The driver half drew the window and then pulled it up and turned his face like there was a disturbing appearance in my direction. Looking back and seeing none, I gestured to him that behind me was just a towering building and he need not worry. I bent. Our eyes met. Then he mumbled something and the car sped off like it was going to save the life of its mother in-law.

In cab two: we were now speeding past Leeds Polytechnic.

"How is Nigeria?" she asked me with a smile that you could pick off her lips with a blade of grass. I had now got accustomed to a smile of this species. I could now comfortably go through it, even rewind and forward it with my eyes shut. I remember the first time I had set foot in the 'developed world,' I had smiled with black generosity. But the more popular response I had often got had always made me wonder if I was using the wrong toothpaste or if I had, in my usual hastiness, worn my shirt inside out. Mmh!

Later I woke up to my reality and I had to try to live to the adage of being in Rome and doing as the Romans. And in an attempt to master the art of peeling the smile, twice I missed my lectures because I was in the mirror rehearsing. But every time I had milked myself dry for it, my smile presented like I was winking at a neighbour's wife. But I persisted and now I may as well declare myself a consultant on this thing; nothing in front of you should intrude on your mind or heart. Then you sniff inaudibly as if there's an insect on your nose. As a matter of fact I have been surprised with the amounts of time I have saved from other species of developing smiles. I now use these chunks of time in more productive areas such as reflecting on life and such things as the smile and interpersonal relationships.

So when she smiled I also peeled off a little like a calculating he-goat as I contemplated the better answer to her question. How is Nigeria? Now that in Europe Africa was a remote approximation where Nigeria was Africa and Africa was in Nigeria and all Nigerians were hopefully Africans, I set to put the record right.

"I am a Musamia son of a Mulukhya from Samia-Bugwe in Busia in Uganda." I said calmly, as I turned to adjust my seat belt.

"That is exciting!" she said. For some reason, I felt at home with the sound of it. Satisfied with my seat belt, I turned towards her with a home smile but I found my friend staring ahead unaffectedly. My heart sank. For some unclear reason, I felt hurt. Emotion over-stretched my tongue.

"So what is exciting?" A frown pulled down my face like it was bearing a basket of mud.

"Wonderful!" she answered picking off a speck from the driving wheel. I almost laughed. What is wonderful?

But this question stuck between my teeth, gritted in fathomless contemplation.

"How is Idi Amin?" she asked, lighting a cigarette.

"Quite healthy! Just been addressing an OAU Conference in our capital city."

"Yes the capital! O.E, you said. And where is that?" she said discontinuing a yawn that threatened to keep her jaws apart for a longer time.

"Bamako!" My eyes were on her face. She concluded the yawn with the tail of a tune she was humming.

"Great!" she coughed and swallowed something. Her head nodded. "Yes, Bamoko, great city! Not so?" There was something she could not find in her pockets. Then the third pocket clutched its lip around her hand. Meanwhile I was burning with an answer to a question I was expecting from her. But my friend was quiet like a corpse.

"Is he still putting people's heads in the freezer?" she popped, braking by the traffic lights. The question had finally come. I lowered my voice to avoid being picked up by Idi Amin's Intelligence apparatus. For it was said that, in Saudi Arabia where he had taken refuge after being deposed over a decade ago, his tail had continued to twitch for the bottom of Uganda.

"He pokes out the eyes of most of his victims –"

"Horrendous!" she exclaimed.

"And so the heads cannot find their way to the freezers." I finished. But my friend missed this because of some tight-fisted cigarette lighter. She cleared her voice and swallowed what had remained.

The car phone bleeped and she rapped a few codes and hang up. Then she mingled us through a juggle of turnings and by the time we emerged onto some likeness of a main street, I could not figure out whether I was in New York or Berlin.

"Brilliant!" My friend burst out like a seedpod in a hot tropical afternoon. This jolted me like a tickled rib. Had it been on one of those days when the stomach brews from a potato feast, there was a very fat chance of developing a *puncture* in my rear.

"Amin was a good student of his Imperial Master!" I wanted to compliment her when I noticed the taxi entering the train station.

"Excuse me!" I said, "I told you the coach station!"

"Oh, shit!" she apologized.

Her bypass had added me an extra three pounds on mileage. I contemplated a heart attack: three pounds would fetch a good Five thousand Ugandan shillings plus, with which if I landed on the village, it would fetch me a place in the folklore till the next Christmas. Yes, an elder would spit some blessings on my chest. I would still even have a balance for a whole bar of washing soap for our chest. But before I could protest, I remembered that I had not paid Thatcher's Community charge and so with our smile, I concluded, "Fantabulous! Isn't it?"

Mid morning

I found a coach had been waiting. I could tell by the impatience in its voice. I looked at my watch. I was just two minutes late. The driver smiled and I mumbled to him in apologetic poise: "East African standard time!" and he answered my greeting with a nod.

The bus was now moving. My briefcase surprised me when it fitted on the rack. I was now wrestling with my jacket. One of those holes in its inner lining had for some reason chosen to understudy a net. Thank God I had just had a breakfast with a carbohydrates bias. My popping elbow missed a sharp nose. It was more due to reflex action on his part than the in-elasticity of my hand.

The bus was hot like a kitchen. I think it was my haste for it that had generated the supplementary heat. Beneath my armpit, I could feel rivulets of perspiration flowing down my body and soaking into the shirt. My hankie also decided to hide. I remembered ironing and putting it in the pair of trousers the night before.

God! I realized that after all I had again worn the wrong pair of trousers; the yellow one with a dead zip. I cannot help remembering the day of its death when it went down with a slice of my skin, firm between its gritted teeth. Someone had to do something, for; literally, I was now choking with vapours of sweat steaming from my body like a medieval steam engine.

"Would you mind taking a seat please!" Looking up, my eyes revealed a man who would have passed for the General Manager of Uganda People's transport. But here he was nothing more than a ticket inspector. I nodded to him as I pinched some toilet paper from the inner pouch of the briefcase. And I wiped my face. But then most of the tissue went missing between my face and my palm.

Then as I bent to sit next to a man whose looks I chose to forget immediately, our eyes met and I decided to move to another seat. The look on the people's faces, this time, as I roamed the corridors of the bus was twisted with frowns in various conditions. I think I'd been about, like a giraffe's pregnancy, too long. Then a lady smiled at me and moved in a manner that I understood. So I gambled and felt free beside her.

"Are you okay?" She meant her question. I nodded. She looked at me again: more in the face this time. I also revenged with one in the middle of her forehead. Hers drained mine. It had the other kind of seriousness. My worry was that I might have turned white. Not that white was bad but that how then would I revert to black?

"And are you going to see a doctor?" There was care in her tone.

Then my heart sank. I must have boarded the wrong bus. I could as well be heading for Iceland or even Kuwait. This is Europe and here anything is possible. For I know of a fellow who had left his studio in a Paris hostel to buy chicken wings but had ended up on an *Inter-city* to Berlin.

Fool! Why didn't I ask? Then suddenly, the light in the coach came on full and all was night outside as the coach went underground and my heart fell, *puuh!* And when I looked through the window, what I saw castrated my heart. Where could I have got all these from? My face looked as if a duck had been incubating on it! I ran my hand over it and I harvested a warehouse of toilet tissue.

I surrendered and accepted her hanky and so, we became friends. We talked like turkeys, all the way to Manchester. Then my bladder began entering third stages of labour. Although the driver said what he said in English, she had to translate it for me into English: it was simply a short brake.

Someone knocked on the door of the toilet and I woke up. A black face intruded.

"Are you Mr... I mean are you the African going to Chester?"

I nodded with an open mouth.

"Ah brother, you have let us down!" he was shaking his head like a goat with clots of hungry flies on its ears. Then, I heard the engine of a bus starting and the gentleman pointed in the direction of the sound. I followed him, and overtook him into the bus. He was still pointing at his luggage then to the driver then to the boot. But the driver looked at him, then at his watch and then climbed on the accelerator. Later I learnt that the black guy was a Mbongeni from South Africa. That he had a flight to catch that afternoon.

Early afternoon.

"I tried all these toilets —" and then the lady stopped, concealing her disgust. Anyway, in brief, she had met Mbongeni and asked him to fish me out of one of those loos. So as the South African smelt one toilet after another, the driver was declining her request to board luggage of an absentee passenger. That was when she saw me overtaking Mbongeni.

What bothered me was not that Mbongeni must have been cursing me. For I knew that if he was as responsible as he had briefly demonstrated, then he should be in some kind of transport to wherever he was to board that plane of his from. What bothered me was the item I was concentrating on when that Mbongeni interrupted me: the graffiti on the walls. There was this particular one of a lady inviting a willing male to a pre-sex romance, of raw buttocks thrashing, as an appetizer for the real course. The address she gave looked genuine. Another one read and answered its question, "Why did God give women legs? To walk from the kitchen to the bedroom." And beneath it, the chauvinist was humbled with a back-bouncing arrow in human dung, "All who scribble on toilet walls are shit!" and then another and another and finally I had forgotten to off load the burden of my bladder.

But how do you tell a lady that you were reading sayings in human dung? I sighed and looked through the window. And reversed the clock back, in time, to Moscow. The year was 1988. We were going to Pyongyang in North Korea for the Thirteenth World Festival of Youth and Students when one in the troupe had kept a bus waiting for over an hour. He explained two months later that a Russian toilet had held him up. That everywhere he turned; he saw village size-mirrors revealing every part of his body.

Anyway, the point now was to clear my name. An improvisation came to mind and I clutched on my tummy. She gasped.

" A stomach upset. Happens at this time after every two months,." I explained. She went still. And I added, "It will go by itself. It runs in the family," I healed and rested the matter.

I was feeling hungry. I wanted to get to Chester quickly. She told me I had less than two hours. Then each of us thought our own things and romanced with the view outside.

Then she wondered how I could not know Mbongeni. "But he is from Africa!" I chose to smile back and she apologized.

"I understand!" I said turning towards the window again. The gardens of snow stretched like cotton fields and my feet itched for warmth.

She said they were beautiful. I agreed. Finding nothing more to talk, we looked at each other awkwardly, like undecided he-goats. And on a bailing instinct, she opened her bag and scooped out a copy of the *Sun* paper and called my attention to a scandal in the Royal house.

"You have a King?" she asked with the curiosity of an overgrown African child being introduced to the alphabet.

"Someone killed ours and left behind some kind of a republic," I answered.

We laughed the whole way to Chester.

Late afternoon
Now in Chester, the heavy drizzle and the thick

overhead cloud muffled the day to near night. The winds were angry and the cold felt for warmth in my open ears. I put my hands over them like I was in a metal workshop. Then when I was just lifting the receiver to call 55 Hool Road, Cathy's voice held me.

"Egesa!" she was approaching.

It was a homecoming to feel a handshake so warm, a breast quilted with care, a smile with tender affection. The embrace and the kiss warmed the numb of the journey and the mean pride of racial prejudice. On impact, Cathy opened to me a depth of warmth that may sustain this body for winters to come.

At 55 Hool Road I met her mother, Elisabeth; warm like baby's porridge and immediate like a hiccup. "Egesa, you are welcome!" At first I thought her an elder sister to her daughter; a paragon of humility whose enchanting smile embarrassed formality. A handshake that rocked my heels is what I got from this mother of the age-mate of my mother's daughter in-law.

"Is there anything you want?"

I told her I was all right. A young girl in her late teens entered and mumbled a greeting, the tail of which remained in her mouth as she immediately got on with her business. My hand was left hanging in the air with half embarrassment before flapping down on my lap like a banana leaf chopped off the stem.

I was told that she was Diana, Cathy's younger sister.

Diana played with Elisabeth like a cat and a kitten

until the chair, which I shared with them, danced like a vehicle on potholes. It was a game of fingers and giggles in which the daughter accused the mother of breaching the rules of the game. They paused for a respite, poised like fighting cocks, as I emptied my second offer of coffee from Cathy.

"Egesa, let's play!" Elisabeth invited me. At first I thought my ears had lost their mind. Then she confirmed their sanity and I blushed. How do I begin this? With my fingers? And which finger? Or with a giggle? And a giggle through my teeth or the nose? My eyes locked with Cathy's and a feeling turned her hand towards the coffee.

"I am feeling rather cold!" I heard myself saying. And Cathy stepped in as a matter of fact.

"Some coffee?" I took the coffee.

Grandchild of Nyanga, I hope you are not thinking of playing with your friend's mother. The voice came back with a menace. It always puts its foot in my way especially when it is jealous of some mischief I am about to relish in. But I am always grateful for it when tides subside.

So I answered it, "But I am in England?"

"Which England?" the voice was already impatient.

"The England you hear about," I felt mature enough to attend to my instincts.

"You boy!" There was now real anger in it. "You are still a child of the soil. Crossing the seas does not hoist you above the tribe." So I listened. "Among us, a mother with a daughter old enough to be your girlfriend is not just anybody. Or do you have a he-goat to *cough*?" This last bit relating to a ruminant sent me choking. I wrestled with laughter when I imagined myself at Heathrow clearing a sacrificial he-goat, pointing one horn ahead of a bell of a testicle, all fresh from a British Airways Boeing. What a sexy way to disembark!

I joined the others for another coffee. A young man, who was introduced as Diana's boyfriend, joined us and fitted at table without ceremony. I will call him "Minus shame" for now, partly because nobody remembered to introduce him. And for reasons of economy, I could as well summarize him simply as, "Minus."

As if Minus had not just arrived a moment ago, he whispered something into Diana's ear and immediately settled to plucking her like a trough zither. His instrument teamed with feeling. And the way he did it, each of his fingers must have had a heart of its own, and a large one at that. She turned and made those other kinds of sounds, like they were only two and-mmh! Cathy watched like they were a pair of deaf and blind jugglers. A male finger licked the air in front of Elisabeth's nose and she pulled her head back like one trying to subdue a fowl with wild wings. She edged away towards me and I edged towards the edge. "Minus, watch out!" Diana gasped. Anyway, the truth is that she called his real name, but breathlessness muffled this dear name and I could not make out what it was. "That is mother if you must be reminded," she playfully cautioned. But Minus was not done with his thing. Now this very fellow was also beginning to breathe funny. This kind of thing through the nose. I must admit I started getting worried. And because he was as crumpled as the upper side of his trousers, I could not rest my fears. Minus was now so near Elisabeth they could exchange their breath.

The first thought I toyed with was to pull this Minus fellow to the door and rest him in the winter outside. But then the voice came back. "What are you dying for?" So I rested and watched the show, live.

Cathy's father just continued about his business; picking more faggots and feeding the fire at a tourist pace, poking the flames indifferently while a man from another clan was feeding his fingers on his own daughter, in his own house, and just next to his wife!

I accepted another coffee with a sigh: well, such is the world and its peoples: cows are rustled in Karamoja while in India, the Hindu worship them.

The atmosphere had become so oppressively unpredictable. What upset me was that I could neither tell what was coming nor how I should react. This chill of helplessness and vulnerability numbed me. And outside, the winds continued to whisper behind my back and beneath a cold cloud. A suspicious uncertainty besieged me and twisted my eyes towards the fire and I got transported to my childhood, when granny would tell us fireside stories; stories with many songs. There was this particular one about a young man who began by looking the elders in the eye. But as the tune of its song began to unfold, Elisabeth woke me up with a start, "Are you married?" This ambush was covered by another offer of German chocolates, which other Englishmen in the room seemed not to give a damn about. I wondered what of theirs the Germans ate. Mmh!

"Not yet." It was a weary answer from me not out of doubt of my marital status as of the colour of the next question.

"What type of girlfriends do you like?" It was Elisabeth still asking. Nobody had ever asked me this question. Not even myself. By the way, who was my type of girl? I tried to flip through my fingers but they thawed into a lethal fist. The only thing that came to mind was the other girl, the one who took off with a butcher. I fought with laughter.

"Any–" my lips had started without consultation. They had wanted to say anything. The question had seemed as simple as water for washing potatoes and yet I had stammered a gap of silence that made me feel more stupid than a donkey. I hated this feeling of naiveté and my delay in answering the question made me feel sick and hateful and angry and- like a horse was hoofing on my tongue, my liver, my manhood, my everything. But certainly, what I had almost said, was even worse; a symptom of unrehearsed instincts, a betrayal of self, country and the whole of that continent.

Elisabeth, Diana, Cathy, the father and the itching Minus were all looking at me. Their eyes filled my mouth. I felt the heat in my liver. I was sweating. I tried to steel myself by dismissing it a simple matter, which an African eligible for a British Visa should be able to weather. But this was just on the surface. Inside, I was sweating blood.

"Some coffee?" Cathy was still beside me. I sighed. I was feeling like throwing up.

"Well," I composed myself and trying to reclaim my dignity, I began at royal pace. "On your question about my type … ah," I coughed a bit but quickly stopped because in my own ears I was beginning to sound as ridiculous as one dancing waltz on horseback. "The lady with personality moves my heart?" Inquisitive doubts mingled their brows. "I am supple to those who do not do the talking for me."

She asked for pardon.

"In brief, I do not mingle well with jingle bells!" I said.

Cathy smiled as if in compliment for an obviously unrehearsed performance, well executed though. I sighed, feeling I had got back part of myself.

Evening

But there are some people who cannot be impressed just like that. This, I learnt when Cathy took Jimmy, a course-mate, and me to get acquainted with some spots in Chester that evening. By the constellation of eyes and the traffic that paused in its path, I seemed the first black eclipse to happen in this English enclave. I was a tourist sight in Chester. My eye turned like a chameleon's. My smile joined both ears with the generosity of a newcomer who imagines everybody is waiting to see him. Then rain, from nowhere, suddenly started urinating in my cup of *pomp*.

God loves His people and so He sent a handy bus. Cathy entered first; Jimmy followed stepping where she had stepped.

"For three, please!" Cathy said and picked her ticket and walked in, Jimmy picked his and walked in and I stretched my hand for a ticket from a driver, who knew too well his routine to mind faces. His face froze as my hand revealed a nocturnal pigmentation and he jerked with the tickle of a sensitive part. Our faces met and an experience kneaded his face. Then a smile on his upper lip knotted this forehead. I appreciated his asthmatic breath and the tan of his skin with an indigenous smile and followed my hosts.

I found Cathy and Jimmy had taken their places in the bus. I did not have any problems with room. I must say that I almost felt embarrassed with the amount of space I, a mere visitor, got in a public means of transport. I felt so touched when even children, old men and women and particularly people of my age rushed out of the way as I approached creating more room. I was just a simple black fellow and yet they continued to curdle their bodies one after another against the feverish frame of the bus until at one point I started to fear the bus would burst out of human pressure like the proverbial mother-chameleon. So I hastened to my seat and when I sat the bus sighed. And just how swiftly a mind works overwhelmed me; every hand reached for the nearest window and opened. It was a sort of mini-Olympics. As for fresh air, I did not have any problem with that. For as bodies touched skin-to-skin at the front, I had a seat to myself. A hurricane of fresh air gushed in. All just for my health. And I was so grateful for this humanity. This was sincerely too much. I had the whole rear seat to myself. And so many kind fellows, packed like mackerels bending like sorghum stems in a storm. Even humility needs taming.

With this space, air and comfort, my mind wandered off to the day of my childhood when we had killed a juicy drake and after unfeathering it, a dog was found having eaten one of its wings. And our father had left all of it for the dog saying men should not bite where dogs have bitten. Now in Chester for the first time, I was acknowledging how that dog must have felt, enjoying all that chunk of a duck, all to itself. And just a wagtail at that!

The bus was speeding like it was going to save its mother in-law. But I did not know the destination. Cathy bent backward and continued to rap to me the sights we were seeing.

"I'm most delighted with the places and the people. Cathy, I feel so honoured." I had courteously answered without recalling a single one of the names. The bus driver looked behind, I saw him, and he smiled with his upper lip and stepped onto something. The bus accelerated as if it was running on six legs. From my window, I could not clearly view where we were going because tense human bodies had now jammed the front of bus. The necks and heads of those nearest to me were frozen with creaking consciousness. Their hair blowing out like a contest of sisal skirts. At one moment I got this silly feeling that if I said *bah!* - these silly thoughts cross every healthy mind I suppose - they would all scream, bursting out through the roof of the bus.

Then there was this Blondie in front of me. That was

the fourth time she was taking it upon herself to tease my comfort by giving that eye of a co-wife. Mmm! I wondered what was in her heart. Being relaxed I also looked at her and saw a pair of eyes, a pair of lips, a pair of ears and two fraternal buttocks, for they did not measure quite a pair. As if they were under the strap of some rude thong. But they were still buttocks anyway; after all there are those who want but do not have them. So hers were still buttocks even if one seemed up a ladder and the other downstairs. They were still buttocks, and her buttocks. Yes just two buttocks like the ones I myself was also sitting on.

"That is how you feel. That is your attitude," the voice told me. And you cannot imagine what she is feeling. She has a right to what she feels in any case. But look here, I found myself answering from within. The labour pains that gnaw the beggar's wife are no less tense than the ones that massage the pelvis of the rich man's wife. Something mingled her upper lip and the blonde turned away. I sighed.

"Egesa!" Cathy called rising as the bus came to a stop. At first, the bus had looked small but as I walked out, I was honoured with such more space that a clan of *Otole* dancers could have performed a complete war motif without scratching anybody.

Outside I found myself confronted with a guard of honour to inspect but before I could salute, something must have happened and the *guard* scrambled into the bus like chicks evading a kite. The communal sigh I heard from inside was what must have started the bus in that gear. A

69

galaxy of eyes pored through the misty glass panes like a hundred packs of hyenas closing in on a carcass. I waved to them.

Cathy looked at me with uncertainty and, as if out of politeness, asked how the ride had been.

"Brilliant, Cathy. It was gorgeous. Wonderfully scintillating!" I retorted with the smile.

After supper, we watched the telly. I made up my mind to keep indoors till my return to Leeds. But at dinner, I noticed that Diana never looked at me. In fact I thought she had avoided my eyes enough times to prove that she was not just shy. We met three times in the corridors and three times she turned away like a bride who had met a father in-law. So when Elisabeth suggested that I go and visit an English pub, I thought of allowing Diana some space in the corridors, she certainly needed it.

Night

It was rather a chilly walk but we arrived in good form. Here everybody did his or her thing like a choir of the deaf. The activity was multiplicative. The music seemed as if it did not want to be left out. The air was thick. You could carve a chunk of it with a blunt knife. The nimbus of cigarette smoke and the odour of liquor suffocated the air as we waded through the bog of humans. The bodies stank with perspiration: expensive perfumes, stinging deodorants, slimy armpits that had spat out water and rancid underwear clogged with genital waste exuded their pungent odour.

Numerous multinational bank notes smeared the counter with a murky international representation albeit not reflected in the clientele.

As I sipped my orange juice, I felt the zoom of eyes cringe my skin. On my right side was a window the size of a six-seater dining table. The night outside was a perfect sample of a night. It could safely deliver a night dancer to your doorstep. Against this background, the low light in the pub was augmented, polishing the window into a mighty mirror that painted both the object and shadow to religious detail. The action was thick. It gave the likeness of the heart of an anthill. The activity here was that of worker termites. Here apart from an eye or two I was still feeling, everybody went about their business, oblivious of trivialities or differences.

True community spirit, I told myself. It was like African folk working the soil in preparation for the planting season. And that is why work and life continues in an anthill. However much an intruder may attempt to dig it up, life continues as long as the heart, the Queen mother is alive.

And as I was about to toast in self-appreciation I realized that there was someone who was not working; she was watching. She was still looking at me. Her features were as prominent as the midday sun on the equator. The face was shaped like a heart. The eyes outstanding, innocent and sleepy supple like a calf's: a deep navy blue; sexy as sexy. The baby face conspired with scarlet lips and her snow-white dress intimately feeling her own body...

71

"God must have settled on you after a good meal," I sighed, the smile I did not show resting in her dimple. The fire in your eyes can inflame the wettest of blankets. Something in me was beginning to stammer.

My mouth was still open when Jim shook me hard by the shoulder. I later learnt they had been calling me for some time. A little embarrassed, I sought nerve in my glass only to realise that it was Jim's glass I had picked instead. Much of the wine had already gone down my throat; and the wrong way. I choked and coughed. It was alcohol for the first time.

"Oh, shit!" I cursed like an American.

Cathy offered me another glass of orange.

The other lady was still looking at me and she winked, "accept", and before I could assent, Cathy was out for it. I swore to ignore her.

But fate stirred my inside and panned my face left before tilting it up and zooming into her. And for another time I caught her eye still locked on me. Once an accident, twice a coincidence and thrice, a habit and habit is next to nature - the heart somersaulted.

My eye missed Cathy by a needle's margin and I toyed with my glass like a home girl nibbling blades of grass at the roadside as she avoids the eyes of somebody's son who insists that he cannot go back to his hut unaccompanied.

To keep my nerves together, I angled away to an unobtrusive position. I faced the mirror and my heart fell! The whole woman and Cathy and Jim and me; we were all in there in the mirror. And they were watching me. They had been watching me. They must have been seeing me all along. My God! But she still looked at me, looked at me until I almost cried out my mother's name.

"I think she was a hard-core prostitute. How can a woman look at a man like that?" I later confessed to Jimmy and Cathy as we walked back to 55 Hool Road.

"Egesa, she is a human being like you and she only wanted you:" Jim had sobered me. I woke to his point and felt more stupid than before.

"She just wanted you!" he had concluded it. But why did I make such an empty observation. I felt like pulling out my tongue or at least a tooth as a token of embarrassment.

Day two: (Mid morning)

This was my last day and place of visitation and I was warming up for departure. So, as we walked towards Chester Zoo, something had struck me. This was the night before. It was not what I had seen on the telly but something about the audience: parents and their children.

It was a film about a man who had avenged his elder brother's ingratitude by raping the latter's bride. The valour with which the grieved fellow executed the vengeance was nothing short of a distress call. At one time, honestly, I felt like the telly receiver was steaming with the heat of the action. What ate my inside was not that it happened but that a family of parents and their children had calmly watched it and drank the scene.

"Wait, mm.! I think he is going to do it…Yes mm!

He is doing it!" Diana honestly voiced over. I plugged my ears and beseeched the most mindful of my ancestors to fetch a descendant. 'No body will bother you for a visa' I muttered to the ancestor. But it seemed like the ground had also closed it ears in embarrassment.

Afternoon into Day Three evening.

Now we had just entered the zoo. We stood at the tiger cage. The tiger there made me feel out of place. It was always on the move like a dog had licked the soles of its feet. It could not settle on its bottom for even a minute. Kept prancing the length of the fence like a racing horse on rehearsal. Whenever it would reach the point of the fence where I was watching it from, it would stop and eye me with a wet mouth. Because I did not know how strong that fence was, I suggested to Cathy that we try the chicken family or the monkey fraternity.

Next it was a Chimp. This one seemed to recognize me well. But honestly, I could not remember us meeting before. Anyway, the most important thing was that it noticed me and immediately changed its behavior as if I was on the wrong side of the cage. It gave me this funny eye of "Traitor!" like I was having a go at liberty while turning a shoulder to those in need; the incarcerated. But honestly I was neither responsible for our relative position nor could I do anything to improve the circumstances; I was just a mere visitor.

Then like a head-pecking serpent it flew at me. Thanks to the one who anticipated our meeting and put a strong glass between us. But its anger was unmistakable. Its anger seemed to ferment.

"Bro. How can you let this continue while you roam in freedom?" That was the face. Honestly, I was getting rather apprehensive and did not like it. And suddenly *Pwah!*, there was another attack on the glass, in the cage behind me and then in front and then behind. A tropical storm had brewed from nowhere and a kid's voice screamed, fleeing the attacker behind me. I turned immediately just in time to face a little lad frightened and ranting for its mother. My face made the situation worse; the kid really fled for dear life. The disarray outside the cage sent the apes fleeing to the safety of the inner cages. The child's mother grabbed her child, curved it in her arms and protectively retreated, her face straight in my eyes; watching me closely.

I turned to face her. By the look on her face, it was obvious that the slightest movement from where I was and the lady would just scream. At this rate, the National Express was going to lose a lot of revenue if it continued attempting to bring wildlife nearer to the people. I turned back to the window. The moon was full and high, rising beyond the canopy of the lightlands. It curved out like a virgin's breast. As the *National Express* curved from lane to lane, the moon danced a solitary dance; a lonely moon in an indifferent sky. But its warmth was there: the warmth of the beautiful memories of Chester.

Chicken Bone

I loved chicken and everyone knew that. So when my grandfather crossed my path, everybody knew a fatal mistake had been made. To be more precise, I had watched his razor canines for some time until he entered the last phase; polishing the leg bone of the chicken with his teeth. Leaning on my left buttock, I edged forward shielding Popi. Popi became uneasy. His movements were those of a cat's tail waiting for a rat. I peered into the face of grandfather; the glint from his eyes was stinging. I narrowed my eyelids a little and waited. Then he wrapped his tongue round the ball of the bone. He then spun it over the bone rinsing it marble white.

A foot stepped on me and I jerked backward only to find Popi in front of me. How ingenious! Living things can be so creative when faced with food, I now came to believe. My stomach was already hurting, hurting for that bone, holding that soup of marrow. The bone. So behind Popi, I toyed with advantage. Realising I was the taller of us, I bent, supported myself on my hands and stood up behind him. That is when I realised that things might have changed pretty fast for I noticed that Popi's head was moving like a slow grinding stone. And true Grandpa's hand was empty. And when I took on a more frontal angle I saw Popi's mouth. Popi's mouth was dripping with wet marrow.

"How could he!"

Mother must have heard my voice from her kitchen, which was only two football fields away. Possibly it was the shrill voice of Popi as he turned and twirled from the effect of the granite stone that had immediately twisted his nape; that stone that I had kept close by my sitting place. Or it could have been *Apala,* the spotted goat, that stubborn he-goat that always took advantage of any slight shift in the atmosphere to sever its rope and run towards home. It may have even been the mug of porridge that I had declined to accept in exchange for the bone; that cup with which my hand also made contact, congesting my grandfather's nose. It was possibly the resulting sneeze that threw the birds off the trees that mother could have heard.

For I met her, halfway at that junction next to the shrub where I met Uncle Amigo trying to urinate on the head of a gecko. Mother ruffled in her black polyester gown, her brown mingling stick angled in anticipation.

"Grandpapa took a bone from my little son, how dare he?" she asked, her hands making two triangles on her sides. Her mingling stick was laced with the *obusuma* she must have been kneading a while ago. She must have left the bread burning on the heath.

"It was a bone of chicken, mother."

"A chicken bone from my little son?"

"Wuwii wuwii!" I sprinted on spot, then made small swift circles and then stamping my little feet, *ta! ta! ta!* I collapsed, sinking into the overgrown path.

"O my little son, how could they draw a bone from his very mouth? And a chicken bone at that?" as she gathered me like a heap of rags, my once white sweater thick with black jack spikes.

"Wuwii, oii!" I wriggled like a reptile that had been sprinkled with paraffin, slipping out of her hands, spilling onto the ground and mixing with another carpet of the black jack. "And he gave it away. My bone." I gasped, the white of my eyes eating the brown.

"He gave it to Michael, your brother. How dare he?" again scooping me by the waist but soon losing me to the ground.

"Not to Michael but Popi. To Po-pi!"

"Po- who?"

"Popi. To his Popi!" I was now rolling like a puppy in sand.

"Gave a bone to his dog and not my little son. Did he not know that a grandson at four loves chicken more than a dog at noon?" she said this as she unloaded me into the chicken house, slapping the door behind and turning the lock a second time.

The Birthmark

Mutende could still hear the voices of the people in the courtyard filtering into the growing night. They had been there, drinking since the first roosters returned. He stretched himself, changed to his side and stared into the darkness. Inside him the storm was brewing. He could feel his heart; each beat pounding the papyrus mat like someone working the door of an offending co-wife.

Mutende sighed and with an effort, he turned to another side. The papyrus mat creaked. For every turning he attempted, it creaked like an old metallic door. He could feel the straws lining his body like a corpse that had been fettered to last a journey of hills and valleys. The humpy floor gnawed into his side. Mutende curved himself into a bow and his body shook with arrows of emotion. He felt tingling in his bones and his joints gave way. The world around him filtered in seamless void and he clenched his eyes.

Outside, a wind blew and dusty soil and blades of grass splattered onto the floor. The particles fell on Mutende's face. He did not move. Another push of wind bent the trees in a whistling hush and a lone frog called in the distance.

Kanoti and Odinga were still drinking outside. Kanoti was Mutende's paternal Uncle. He lived across the river in the next village and he was a regular company in this home where he often came to drink in the evenings.

"Odinga, everybody has finished their drink and gone

home except you. I say finish that quickly and we move. It is coming to rain," The words came off Kanoti's tongue like some thick paste.

There was silence.

"I know you are awake and hearing me. I say, am I talking to a monitor lizard?" he continued.

Odinga shifted in his chair and remained quiet.

"And you have been drinking that one glass of *waragi* which has refused to get finished." Kanoti completed the sentence bending and peering into his face.

"Kanoti if you are tired, get up and go back to your home." Namacheke, Mutende's mother shouted, emerging from the kitchen house.

"Why are you always defending him? I am talking to a fellow man. So keep quiet, woman," he bayed.

Namacheke hissed, spat loudly on the ground and entered her house.

"Mm, you think I do not know." Kanoti said wobbling onto his feet. "I say, even if you hiss like a python and spit a river, I will not leave Odinga behind," *bphwrrr...* He belched and retched like a faulty lorry engine.

A window opened in the main house and Namacheke peered with an irritated eye.

"Are you vomiting again, Kanoti?" She had been waiting for long and was getting impatient. She felt like saying something about his limp that made his movement similar to that of a goat with a broken hind leg but she remembered how it happened and thought twice about mentioning it. Surviving a crocodile bite after you have

80

swum to save a drowning mother was an act people continued to talk about despite his regression into drink. And in fact many people, including Namacheke did at times understand him, a man bursting with youth had been reduced to depend on his mother for support after his wife left swearing she was tired looking after the home as if there was no man in it. But like Namacheke had just been explaining to her husband, Kanoti should not be allowed to continue making like difficult for others. Who does not have a problem? He had to be told to leave. She looked through the window and called "Kanoti!"

"I have finished. *Haa* ... *puu*! I say." Kanoti spat again.

The head withdrew from the window and hushed voices could be heard coming from inside of the main house. The tones were high. Namacheke and her husband, Mafulu, seemed not to be agreeing over something.

A small but controlled voice came from the direction of the window. A stranger would have mistaken it for a woman's if s/he had never heard Mafulu speak. "Kanoti, I think you are tired. Go home and catch some sleep. Goodnight, cousin!" Mafulu's tone was gentle.

"Mafulu, go away from that window, I say. Go back to your cold bed and let me settle a matter of concern to our clan." Kanoti barked.

The window banged and confrontational murmurs could be heard inside. Namacheke and Mafulu were sounding more disagreeable. Odinga turned in his chair but did not say anything.

Kanoti staggered to the table, supporting himself on Odinga's shoulder before reaching for his glass of liquor and running it down the throat. Odinga, who was watching him from the corner of his left eye, pulled his cape over the face and did not flinch. He had come to know Kanoti very well. It was wiser not to answer back, or else you'd need to lose some money for boozing him to some state of quiet.

This Odinga was the father of Rose, a girl whom Mutende loved. Rose was Odinga's only child. Odinga had stopped the relationship between Mutende and Rose. He had banned it. Rose was a girl of a different clan. She and Odinga her father had no blood relationship with Mafulu's family or clan. Neither of the families had been associated with some chronic condition in their line. So Mutende had found no basis for Odinga's action. But Odinga had urinated on their plans.

Odinga was so close to Mafulu's family that the children grew up calling him Uncle. It is only later that they realized he was of another clan. Odinga was not a bad man. He would not be a problem if it were not that he was behaving as if the two families were one and related. He had twisted friendship into authority and with this he had separated Mutende from his girlfriend Rose. His action had caused Mutende tremendous misery. Odinga was causing him a lot of pain. And nobody seemed brave enough except Kanoti Mutende's uncle. When drunk, Kanoti would border on dragging Odinga out of the home. And this often pleased Mutende, wishing a crocodile had not come the way of his Uncle; possibly he could have dragged him away eternally.

Kanoti was the only one to insult Odinga and get away with it. And yet Odinga, tough as he seemed, did not answer back Kanoti. It was for himself that Odinga took every care not to cross swords with Kanoti.

And whenever Kanoti got erratic, which he often did, Odinga would buy him booze and they would laugh and talk about a few common things. Kanoti was known to use blackmail to get booze in exchange for good manners.

"Odinga, am I talking to a tree? Eh, I say, did you come to sleep here?"

"Am I the keeper of your legs?"

"It is coming to rain, I say." Kanoti persisted.

"The rain that falls this month does not come from that side. This is a barren wind," Odinga answered with a closing finality.

"Why do you keep rotating in my cousin's home as if the owner were dead? Odinga, you won't leave my cousin room to even fart. I say, what is it that you have not found in your home that you come to look for from Mafulu's. One day you will die and very soon. I say, the food that your wife cooks must be very watery."

"Kanoti, that will be the last beer you are taking from me, if you continue howling like an insane man," Mafulu's voice whined through the window as the door to the main house opened with a screech.

"Kanoti, get out of here, or else I will scatter that banana leaf of a shirt and spread you like cowhide," Namacheke said, approaching.

"Woman, I say, do you want to hit a man with that?" There followed the sound of a jerrycan against the wall. "Why didn't you stay if you thought you were a man?"

"*Ha, phu!* I say, wait until tomorrow, you will know who the real Kanoti is."

A passing wind hummed thinning his words away. Retreating feet could be heard wobbling into the distance beyond Mutende's hut.

There followed a spell of silence outside. Mutende sighed and with an effort turned onto his back. Twinkling shafts of moonlight peeped at him through the cracks in the thatch. He tried to shift his face away from light but his neck would not move. Mutende agonised.

"Why? What is my crime?" He shook his fist at the darkness. But stark silence stared into him. His voice clogged in his throat.

"But what do you gain by feeling so bitter about it and about things that do not go your way?" a voice confronted him. "You are the problem and not anybody else. It is you crucifying yourself on that shallow cross of indecisiveness." the voice continued more intently. "Look here, my friend, you take long to respond and, more often, by the time you do, the tide will have rent your mast."

Mutende nodded. "That is my problem; fearing to hurt people. And that is how I have ended hurting every joint of my life, all my life."

Mutende recalled the words of one of his teachers that life should not be about seeking the satisfaction of self as an end in itself. That the fullness of life should be through the service of God and fellow men.

But his father had been more precise. "Son, as you grow you will find life putting its foot in your way. You will stumble into potholes of conformity, of sacrifice, of pain. Yes, we swallow pain in the name of this life."

And whenever his father reached the tail of this philosophy, his voice would shake and his eyes moisten, glistening with tears. And tonight, as he lay in his bed, those words echoed with a haunting depth.

Mutende swallowed a dry throat and turned to another side. "Why should I let somebody else run my conscience?"

"No. Never again!"

Mutende swore not to move near the bed. Not just the bed, but the bed and the woman on that bed. Yes, that woman and her child on that bed. He clenched his lips and, gnawed his molars. "But that is what you ought to have done when you returned from college to find that your father had married you a wife; without your consent," the voice returned, rekindling memories of that day.

Hardly a month ago, while at college, he received a message instructing him to return home. He found his mother Namacheke, his father and Odinga in the sitting room of the main house. The pressed yellow seat covers that hung on the foldable wooden chairs had been meticulously laid. The blue and red table flowers in metallic vases cut out of insecticide cans told of an event. His aunt who lived in Mawero, a distance from home, was there to receive him. Strange, this one was to him. But before he could ask if some in-laws were being expected, his aunt had hurried out through the door leading to the kitchen.

His father who had been sitting still, thoughtfully, on his three legged stool next to the door, a position that gave him full command of the main entrance into the home, cleared his throat huskily and began, "A neighbour of your aunt came and complained about you."

"About me?" Mutende's mind started running amok.

"Yes! There is a complaint about you," Mafulu said, not looking his son in the face.

"Who was that and what did he complain about?"

"Opondo complained to your aunt that you had misbehaved in his home."

Mutende peered at his father, a quizzical frown wringing his forehead.

"You made his daughter Betty pregnant," he said with a surface seriousness. Mafulu continued to evade his son's face as he said these words.

"What? Impossible!" He sprang to his feet and his father looked him strait in the face. Their eyes stayed in contact and Mafulu moved his hand slowly but firmly. Mutende hesitated and then slowly sank to his seat. A moment of silence. Mafulu cleared his voice and swallowed a dry throat. "Opondo was offended and Opondo is not a child."

"No!" Mutende cried, his eyes widening.

"Mutende, someone's daughter out there got-" Odinga put in.

" I do not know anything about that."

"We are telling you, my son —" Mafulu was visibly struggling to contain himself.

"Impossible!" Mutende slapped his thighs.

"Mutende, what are you saying is impossible? Mafulu cut in, almost shouting.

Mutende stared at his father with an open mouth. There was a pause. Mafulu sighed, "My son, you are no longer a child and I want you to behave responsibly. Now, Mutende, did you at any time visit your aunt?"

"I... did but –?" Odinga slapped a vertical finger over his lips and Mutende held his tongue.

Mafulu opened his lips, closed them without a word and sighed. And in a very measured voice he asked. "While at your aunt's home, did you in any way add yourself to Opondo's daughter as a man would with a woman?"

"Possibly!" he mumbled.

"Possibly?" his father was becoming restless.

"You mean you do not remember?" Odinga barked.

"But –" Mutende was beginning to get angry.

"But what?" Odinga smacked.

"But why won't you let me talk," he snapped like a string. "Do you know the implications of what you are saying?"

"My son, I know more implications than you may be aware of. And that is why, when we got that report of your misconduct, we looked into this matter as parents and managed to settle it as grown up people."

"Father, what and... I mean how did you settle what?"

"As I talk now, the dowry has been settled and your wife and child have been brought home," Mafulu concluded.

Mutende stared at his father. "Thank God," his father hastened. "My grandchild is a boy! And for your information we have already done the naming: he is my father, your grandfather, his great-grandfather Mutende; the warrior," Mafulu said with an empty smile.

"No!" he screamed.

"Yes, he is Mutende, your namesake!" his father said, nailing the "yes" home.

"Why are you doing this to me? How can you do such a thing to someone you call your child?"

"Because I love you and this home. It is because I know more than my child does," Mafulu returned with steeled emphasis.

"You have been framed. That girl is a liar. There is something she is up to."

"My child, Mutende." his mother was hardly audible.

"I am not yet over. She is a liar. It is hardly six months since I met her, how could she possibly have got my child and delivered it?"

"First pregnancies are usually impatient –" Namacheke put in pleadingly.

"No. That is not my child." Mutende turned his back to them.

"Whose is it?" Odinga asked threateningly grabbing him by the shoulders and spinning him to a breath-to-breath position.

"Why don't you go out there and ask her? Why me?" He said waving his arm causing Odinga to retreat slightly.

"We asked Betty, and she said it was you," his father replied very calmly. Mutende attempted to move again but his father signalled him to remain in place.

"Son, you now have a family to care for and you will do well not to offend your parents," his father said, still calm.

Mutende watched his father, assembling those words, in numbing disbelief. He felt like reaching for a chunk of Odinga's mallet head and bashing it into his father's crouch. Deep inside him he simmered with a desire to perform something drastic, to tell them something they would keep in their hearts forever but somehow the sight of his mother poured cold water on his tongue. Her legs folded on a mat, her head angled to the left and cupped in the left palm, tears were streaming down Namacheke's wrinkles.

With the right hand she reached for the crumpled edge of her *lesu* and cleared her nose. She then stretched her legs, bent forward supporting her torso on the elbows and stared into the outside.

Mafulu turned in the chair, cleared his throat and said nothing. Odinga was studying the face of Mutende, looking for symptoms of dissension. There was a chilling stillness. Odinga pushed forward, cleared his throat and angled his forehead like a confrontational he-goat.

Mutende knew Odinga for his persistence. Like a leech, he would stick and only let go when his motive was fully achieved. He knew if he were to win this fight, it would take resilience. The fight would leave behind a cluster of wounds, he anticipated and was ready to pay the price for the marriage to work.

The sight of Odinga made Mutende feel like throwing up in his face for it was this same Odinga who had made a nightmare of his love with Rose. He had taken her away from him and hidden her. She had been hidden a second and possibly last time. The first time they did it, Rose had been smuggled to Kenya and was rumoured to be attending school at Nangina Girls'.

His parents and the girl's relatives had then kept her location secret until a cattle smuggler brought him the news at a cost of what the smuggler called 'a people's fee'. Then, Mutende could only raise half the money and the two agreed that the balance must be paid in a week's time. Arguing that a youth is more likely to follow his heart than his head, the smuggler had promised unfriendly consequences if Mutende did not honour his word. Mutende had laughed, promised and patted the smuggler on the shoulder with the hand of a friend.

Mutende had got in touch with Rose and for the holiday season, they skipped home and rented a backroom in a trading center where they re-united. Meanwhile his parents believed he had remained at college preparing for his final year exams. Mutende and Rose played and made love like they had been issued a license. And they talked of hope, of renewal, of commitment and the approaching marriage.

Then one morning, a week having passed and another day gone, the smuggler friend, having got suspicious of the waiting, had traced one of Odinga's nephews. On the prompting of a higher fee, the smuggler had led the cousins of Rose to their hideout. And what followed immediately involved fists, bleeding knees and a broken nose.

Mutende expected a backlash after watching the siege and reclamation of Rose from an adjacent window, before returning to school to resume his studies. Because he had just gone to buy pancakes before the cousins pounced, they did not find them together and Rose denied that it was Mutende with whom she was. And so she had been warned never to attempt such a thing again, and she promised. And they broke that promise. But he had never imagined that it would lead into an impromptu marriage for him.

Here they were again! And on this day, Odinga seemed dressed for a showdown. Odinga edged his neck forward and focused on him. Mutende looked at them, from father to mother to Odinga and back to where he started and tried to map out who the beneficiary of this new joke of Betty and her baby could be. And as he was still figuring out, three people; his aunt, Betty and Mutende Junior entered through the kitchen door. The aunt was now leading them in.

Mutende went wild; really wild like a bull broken loose after surviving an attempt to slaughter it. His mother wept, beseeched, threatened and implored. Betty had scrambled up from the knee that she had bent in the process of greeting, tumbling and jumping over the baby that found itself spread on its little back. The baby yelled wriggling like a piece of snake that has been chopped off from another part. The shawl went off leaving it completely naked an exposing its protuberant navel the size of a little fist.

The aunt had gathered the baby like a towel fallen off an open body and had scampered off.

But Odinga persisted with a determination that would have passed him for a brother of the girl. With one voice, they had stood their ground; the three of them. She was his wife. He was his son. Period! How can they imagine that I could father such a child with such a big navel when we do not have it in our family? At least if it had a birthmark around that navel like I do, I would possibly-. but he was not given time to even say a word of what was flashing through his mind.

"Didn't you cover yourself with Opondo's daughter under the same blanket, or do you want to tell us that you turned with your trousers on?" Odinga shouted in his face.

"But –"

"But what?" his mother had crossed his tongue, tears drenching her face.

"But don't you see that that baby is mature," he found himself barely pleading.

"Did you want a premature one?" Odinga spat out.

"I did not, and I do not, want any premature gifts," he shot back.

"My son. Some pregnancies are quick. First pregnancies are always like that, they come early."

"I do not love her, mother. I love someone else."

"What has love got to do with marriage?" Namacheke asked.

"A woman is a woman." Odinga said, with steel finality.

Theirs was a deaf determination.

"Take it from me, my child," his mother had beseeched. "In whatever you do and say, think about the name of this home, my son. We are your parents and all we are doing is for you and this home."

"I do not love her and I hardly know her," he looked into his mother's eyes, pleading.

"You may not love her now but you will learn with time. Let her stay. Give Betty a chance," the mother continued. "Take the girl we have chosen for you, my child. Do it for this home."

"For this home?" he asked. He was confused.

"I am now getting tired of this circus. This girl is going to stay and that is it!" Mafulu said stumping his foot hard, slightly losing balance and holding onto the table.

Mutende pranced out with such strides that even the chickens that were feeding on the cassava in the drying yard scattered as if he were a kite.

Namacheke had followed close at her son's heels fearing that he would bring harm upon himself. And when she saw Mutende enter his house and heard a slump of exhaustion on his bed, and the door of the house did not close, her fears were eased. But she kept by her son's hut for long enough to be a little surer.

Namacheke had watched her son closely for about a month. But since that time, up to this day Mutende had sworn not to go under the same blanket with Betty. When she came to the bed, he would move to floor and when she came to the floor he would move out on the veranda and refuse to answer her call.

Since that day they told him she was his wife, he always put on three pairs of underwear and a pair of shorts inside his pair of trousers, all with metal zips. He did not want to be taken unawares just in case he falls very asleep or Betty comes up with some other plan. So as Betty and the child slept on the ground he lay in his bed.

The voice of Kanoti harassing Odinga had long vanished from his ears. For a long time Mutende stared into the roof. He just hated them. He hated them with all the bile in his heart. They had ripped Rose from his breast when they defied Odinga's ban and were in the process of eloping. She was tucked away and now they were casting a dark cloud over him. Who were they to drive him to such an edge? What right did they have to define his path with such impunity? Where does family stop and where does the individual assume?

Mutende recalled how at such trying moments Rose would give him the strength and will to continue. She would often talk about the individual and will in the storm of relatives. She talked about it when they first met. She talked about life, about love and about custom and chains of conformity. At every meeting she would talk about it.

He found Rose a girl who loved and cared. And he loved and cared for her. And he made love to her often, whenever it was possible. As he turned in his bed contemplating this woman they were trying to conscript him into a relationship with, he reminisced about Rose. His mind went back to the night before her cousins had hounded her out of their hideout.

Rose and Mutende had strolled in the moonlight, tracing the edges of the road and straying into the open grassland. And in a short distance, behind a scanty shrub, they had lain and released raw feeling into flesh, letting nature and youth mingle with a passion that numbed and disabled. And down, on the thin grass and warm earth Mutende had sprawled like a spent drake; his feet folded, his knees raised, body relaxed. Mutende was baby naked and with a breeze blowing through his damp bottom, it was cool. His legs wagged gently as if he was doing some fresh air exercise. He was at home.

"Rose," Mutende called, his gaze lost in the serene moonlight sky that he and Rose lay under, their love making having reduced them to a sweet paralysis.

"Mike!"

"Yes!" he answered and waited.

"I thought you called me." Rose added.

"I did."

"I am listening, Mike!" She preferred calling him Mike for that was his Christian name.

"I was just wondering what we should do," Mutende said.

"Do it again; make love to me, M-i-k-e."

"I know I will and when I begin nobody will stop me."

"Mike!" There was a sense of waiting in her tone.

"What shall we do about these people," his voice came but kind of distant. "They do not want us to be together." And he sighed.

"They should not tell us what to do," she was snappy.

"That does not take away the problem, you know."

"Look here, Mike," she sat up, stretched the *lesu* beneath them, leaned on the left hand and touched him gently with her right hand, "we set aside this time for you and me. Let us talk about us, let us be together. Mike, everything has its time. This is our time."

"I was just...thinking. I am sorry." He sighed and their eyes looked into each other. She bent gently. He liked the supple touch of her lips. Just the right amount of salt he thought and he pouted his lips again for another one. But she did not return it. She was looking ahead. He swallowed a wet throat and laid back his head.

"Mike, I believe that whereas we need to respect others' interests, I still think that there is where society must stop and let the individual alone. It is our life and we shall not live it for others," an edge of irritation lining her voice.

Mutende found Rose an intelligent girl. She liked him and she loved him. He liked her and he loved her. They liked and they loved each other. Rose's smile always intrigued him. In it he always felt silver warmth. To Mutende, Rose always sounded older, sincere and honest and for truth always; like she was a blood cousin of faithfulness.

"I often talk to my friends about you," he whispered.

"Which friends?"

He could tell that she wanted to hear it and Mutende

liked that. "My friends at college. I tell them, 'My Rose is the sister to innocence; a smile in humility.'"

"You do!" She edged closer to him and when her hip felt his, she turned and faced him and lifted his head to her knees very gently. The light in his eyes shone in her eyes.

"Rose, that smile touches the very thread of my affection; my humanity."

"Mike that is poetry," she was husky and hardly audible. Mike felt her voice and that was enough for him, not the words.

"That voice of yours has kept its fibre as ever. I still hear and feel it as I first did when we lay in this very spot making our first love, that day I felt the woman in you. Your voice is still there, there in my ears, Rose; cool and natural in its alluring alto. Its silver halo blending with the dark complexion of your mahogany skin, the skin that glistened in the moonlight. That night of our meeting. Rose that night still hangs in the air like morning mist."

"Mike, I am here with you."

Mutende sighed and his torso slumped with the exhaling of air. Rose felt the movement of his body and she edged towards him, slightly. "Mike, touch me... here! Thank you."

"Thank you."

"It's me to thank you."

"It is my hand which is there. So I should be the one to thank you." Pause. "Thank you!"

"Thank you too," and she closed her eyes for a moment then opened them. "Your hand is over stretched. Move closer. Your hand, please!"

"Oh, sorry," he said, adjusting.

"Thank you!" She heard him swallow a wet throat. During the movements he had slipped back to the ground. "Face this way Mike."

"I am still looking at her," he said his eye in the sky.

"The moon?" she was a little on edge.

"Yes, that strip of cloud lacing her oval side. It intrigues me; the bikini cirrus, lighting a naked sky, illuminating an infinity of the dry season terrain. It so calmly fades in the silhouette of the Nambuku hills; filtering into the haze of distance," and he sighed.

"Talk to me, say something about me, Mike."

"I like that moon. Yes, it reminds me of you?"

"Yes Mike, and I am here now, with you. Tell me how you feel now, about me!" She edged on her elbow and supported herself to a sitting position. She began to gently feel the skin of his body.

"Rose. That is good," he said relaxing the muscles so that he could fully feel the touch of her liver-soft hand along his length. Her warm breath over his neck and the descent of her wet tongue started to stir his inside; Mutende closed his eyes and sailed in weightlessness. Then her tongue played, tickling his navel. He liked the cooling effect of her breath on the parts of his skin where her tongue had played.

"Rose, you will make me return here tomorrow." She did not respond to him. Then he first opened one eye, then another. He then opened both of them wide.

There was a silence and when Mike looked close

in her face, he noticed a little dent into the left check. That was her dimple. Deeper this time and he knew she was smiling. He looked in her eyes; they glowed like two diamonds.

"I wonder how some men manage?" he said with surface seriousness.

"Manage what?" she sounded lost.

And he got close and whispered, "An affair without a dimple."

"O stop it, silly boy!" she said giggling, before turning to him and taking his face into her arms. Then she teased "And how about a woman loving a man without dimples."

"Hey Rozie, I have one," and he said "here!" touching the cheek of his left bum, and they laughed and wriggled like happy puppies before he finally ended up on his tummy, the knees down and his bare bottom up. He looked like a little boy left on his tummy in the cradle. He cut a silly posture but she liked it. She liked it when he did crazy things when they were just the two of them. It just made him himself.

She smacked him lightly on his naked bum. He liked the feeling. A wind blew and he liked the refreshing sensation it left as it went through his open bottom. He wagged his bum slightly and let another breeze through. It was most refreshing.

"I like the light from your eyes. It brings out the beads in them. I will kill for these eyes." Then he licked her eyelashes. It was ticklish and she laughed pushing her torso forward, invitingly and he liked the effect. He was moved and he moved her close. "And this one also."

"Mh, they remind me of something."

"What?" Although she knew and had heard it over and over, Rose loved to hear it over and over. She always would wait to hear it. It always reassured her of his feelings towards her.

"They are like a pair of goats' hearts."

"Come on Mike, stop it!" she giggled tenderly edging closer.

"And from this angle they are like two papaws."

"Oh, I hate you!" she struck a mock blow on his chest and threw her neck a little back, propping her chest forward, invitingly.

"My next poem should be about gizzards."

"Gizzards?"

"Yes, and just because – " and she tried to wriggle away.

And the following day the cattle smuggler had led her cousins to their hide out. And after she healed of the bruises from the forced eviction, and promising they would not get together, Mutende swore that he would lay down his life for love and very soon she and Mutende met in the sun, in the rain and under the moon whenever there was an opening. "Whenever I can I will peck you as often as a hen does mother earth," he tugged at her and she reacted as if she was a circuit of live wires. They had heartily chuckled, opening their hearts wide to one another like they would never love again. Their meeting point had become as hard as a school playground. Throwing care to the wind, they had continued to repent of the same sin to the same priest every Sunday till he had told them to come with something different at next penance. Then they had put the priest behind, continuing to meet every evening; changing nest. And when the nephews of Odinga learnt of their rendezvous, they planted thorns on the grounds.

But like lovers, their hearts went over walls and circumvented barricades, mastering the art of evasion from the craft of the hunters. Many times they had met, once in his hut, then in the hut of one of her cousins as he waited to capture them somewhere, then in a bathroom and also twice in the mornings on her way to the garden, on the other side of a thicket. Tired of acting and hiding, the lovers had come out in broad daylight and they had held hands in the view of everybody. Of the two of them, Mutende seemed to care the less. But she was worried.

"My cousins' ways have begun to worry me," she had told him.

"It must be because they do not like me," Mutende said.

"That is not right."

"Eh, are you beginning to defend them?"

"Mike, I have several times asked you to drop that attitude."

"Which attitude."

"That people hate you. It is not you they hate; it is our relationship they do not like."

"That is not news, Rose."

"And so?"

"Mind our business."

"I have to worry, Mike, because they can hurt you and I do not want anything on earth to touch you."

"Mmm! That sounds romantic, Rose," he said, drawing her closer.

"Wait, Mike. It is serious. I think what is causing more concern is the way we are conducting ourselves. I mean this holding of hands and acting as if we do not care about how they feel." He listened. "I see it from the way they look at me. How they now drop tone when they see me approaching."

"It worries you?"

"Mike, I cannot rest. I turn in my sleep and get nightmares of people hacking you to small pieces and disposing of you in different places."

"Rose, don't you think you are just becoming paranoid?"

"Mutende, I know what I am talking about. I feel it. It is real. Recently even my other cousins have begun looking at me as if I was some used sanitary pad. And just yesterday one called me *Namwandu*. Why would he call me a widow."

Mutende's forehead furrowed. The clustered movement of his fingers leaked out an emotion that was taking the better part of him.

"You know what, let us do this," and he edged forward with uncertainty and anticipation as he said thoughtfully.

"We are running away."

"And going where?"

"Wherever the road will lead us," and he rose up.

And so Mutende and Rose had talked and agreed to elope. First she would come to meet him at church and as the people filed for Holy Communion, she would board a *boda boda* bike and join him at the bus stop in the next village. And they would then catch the People's Transport bus to Busia where they would cross to Kenya, buy an engagement ring and quickly marry at the district commissioner's. And after that the rest would look after itself.

On that day, the bus was delayed and Rose's cousins moved faster and soon a crowd had formed and what transpired brought together a whole village.

Odinga had churned with rage; his hands circling over his head like he was warding off a swarm of obstinate bees. "Possibly with another girl, but not my Rose. Upon my dead body, never!"

"But, father, what is wrong with Mutende. What is wrong with us?" Rose cried.

"All will be ok as long as you keep your ways apart." Odinga was breathing hard.

"But-"

"Open that mouth again and I will have that tongue scooped out," he snarled at Rose, moved and narrowly missed her head with a cane picked from a stall he stood next to, the owner having moved from her merchandise and joined the rest in watching what one dubbed 'a free live show.'

"Why do you want to cause your father that anguish?" one bystander asked. "There are many handsome young men around."

"Some of us are here for the taking; free of charge as pig offal," said one young man as he moved his hand narrowly missing a suggestive contact with the bottom of Rose. Odinga picked another cane and lowered it on the head of the offending youth with such style and accuracy that only an insane person would have stayed around without invitation.

"Look, although we have grown up as brother and sister, we are not-" Mutende begun.

"Mutende, where did you leave your ears? If you do not find them, there may come a time when you will not feel strong enough to face yourself in a mirror. You will walk away from light into the darkness and bleed for the sun to die so you may never see your face again," Odinga swore.

Rose could not contain her consternation for this, to her, was nothing but a curse on Mutende. She found herself facing her father, an arm away, his breast heaving.

"What is that meant to be?" she screamed.

He slapped her and soon her cousins had stepped forward. And Mutende watched in disbelief as they lifted her off the ground, her hysterical feet peddling the air and gaining no distance. Amidst this furore, Mafulu his father once again had left the day to Odinga, had locked her somewhere and thrown away the key.

In the evening of the day this happened, when

Mutende's emotions had settled, he had sought and faced his mother.

"Tell me, mother, for a son seeks the real truth from his mother. Is there something you are not ready to discuss about why I should not marry my Rose?"

"Mutende, what are you saying?" Namacheke stared at him

"What is wrong with Rose and me?"

"Son, although you are now grown up and a man, you are still my child."

"What does that mean?"

"I will tell you when you stop looking me in the mouth."

"It is the last time it happens, mother," he said, lowering his eyes.

"As your parents, it is in our interest to advise you on the kind of girl you can have a serious relationship with."

"But this is my life."

"And you are our son, a child in this home. This home must stand."

"What do you mean?"

"You do not understand and you may never understand"

"What do -?"

"Do not ask me any more questions, Mutende," she had said wiping tears, "My son, if it was another girl, yes. But that one, Mmm! Not one from that home," and she shook her head.

The pain in his heart and the faith in love dragged his

knees towards anywhere he thought redress could come. But it was all silent stares. With his grandmother, it was proverbs as usual.

"Child of my child, your elders are older than you. If you have ears use them and use them well. Do not touch that girl again. For a fly that did not heed advice was buried with the corpse."

As Mutende reflected over the events of the day he felt a churning bitterness. He believed himself stupid for having even imagined that his grandmother could contradict his mother. For after all, the granny had always sang praises to her daughter in-law for having given her son children. "As if someone told her that without this daughter in-law of hers my father would not have fathered. How many fertile wombs are out there weeping for child, clotting with seed?"

Mutende loved his father. As a child they had grown up close doing many things together, going to graze cattle together. He told him many stories about his childhood and his great grandfathers. They picked mushrooms together when the season came and peeled ripe papaws with their hands. Once the father shared with him a white ant. Such was the bond between father and son. Mutende was the most hardworking of the children, very welcoming and keen on the welfare of his parents. Many believed Mutende was destined to be heir to his father. Mafulu himself had often hinted at this. Mutende found his father, a man of slight build so contrastingly different from the athletic features of all his children, a man who oscillated between extremes of warmth and introspection. There were moments when he would be withdrawn for days, hardly talking to anyone. Then little Mutende would sit beside him, at times squat in front of him, and look into his eyes and the little boy's eyes would drown in tears. During such times, his father would take him by the hand, wipe away Mutende's tears with the edge of his shirt and they would walk, the two of them, for long distances. Some times he would tell him stories, some times they would just walk. And he would pick him fruits from trees or take him to the swamp and uproot sugar cane for him. And they would carry some for the brothers at home.

Mutende found Mafulu a good father. He was a good father to him and he liked him except for one big flaw; easily giving in on many vital issues and letting his mother single-handedly run the home. Nothing would be done without her seal. And Odinga was her ear. His was the last word. Odinga had taken over their home. Always exploiting proximity to undermine, this is how Mutende saw him. A jealous man sees the world through a jealous heart. Mutende knew Odinga to be so jealous as not to stomach seeing his daughter, Rose, in a happy relationship. Thinking of it now, Mutende could not recall a single night that Odinga did not hang around the home till nearly everybody had gone to sleep. How blind could his parents continue to be? Couldn't someone out there tell Odinga enough is enough? Couldn't someone out there at least tell him to leave Mutende and Rose alone? But Rose had been whisked away to a destination that was difficult to access.

He had gone up to Nagina Girls School to look for her and found she was no longer there. And people remained indifferent and quiet.

Apart from Kanoti's occasional tirade, the only person from whom Mutende registered some concern was his only aunt. Uncoiling him from the misery of his cross-border loss, and the scuffle when they physically lifted her away into final hiding, his aunt had invited him to recuperate at her home in Mawero. Then she had, somehow, introduced him to a girl from the neighbourhood. "She is a good girl, respectful, abiding, hardworking and she comes from a family of people. She is Betty."

And so Mutende had met with Betty on the second night of his stay. After a familiar ritual of the traditional "tug of war" they had wrestled themselves into mutual positions and together, they had shared intimately. His feeling of relief could have lasted a little longer had it not been that she suffered morning sickness and threw up on his chest early in the morning. When he accused her of poor indigestion she had instead put the blame on what she called his persistent manner before leaving him in a crumpled bed and marshy mess. He just sighed and ticked it off as an occupational hazard. Although he found himself in the fling, he knew he was just passing time.

Why a pastime? Now, his past was breathing into his face with fumes of garlic. Mutende felt so disappointed with himself; that he had again fiddled with his own life.

Then he began to wonder if his was not just a weakness of nature, the folly of a heart in pain, desperate for anything, for relief. And relief had brought him what had now grown a tail and a head: a woman and a child now lying with him in the house. And as if at the prompting of his thoughts, the baby began to whimper, and then it suddenly burst into a shrill cry. It was so sharp and Mutende was already exhausted. He found his fingers and traced his ears. He plugged his fingers into his ears. He closed his eyes tight to avoid the sound.

Outside, nocturnal sounds – Kanoti's voice too had faded with the night. Subdued voices came from the direction of his parent's house. Mutende felt one alternative left for him: tell his parents that he would not take that Betty and her baby. He would leave the home and go anywhere; anywhere away from the woman, the child and them.

And he had to tell them that now, and get it over with. He closed his eyes, steadying his mind. He started to count from one to infinity, a trick they always used at school to fight insomnia and by a certain figure, that one often would not recall the following morning, one would be transported to sleep. So Mutende began from one and then to the next, the next and the next after the next after the next. And soon he was off, snoring like a cat. He did not even hear that piercing voice of the baby nor could he feel the touch of Betty as she implored him to fetch some warm water to give to the baby for its gastric contortions.

Mutende was now in another world. In this world, the time was day. His parents were there. Odinga and some of his relatives had assembled too. They were sitting in the courtyard as he approached. And when they saw him, they all rose in what seemed like defensive formation. Mutende steadied his breath to keep his composure. For he needed it; at least initially. The words had to be as clear. "A child is not fathered by allocation but through sperm or adoption. And the child in turn belongs to the home, which the father belongs to."

No sooner had he said this than Namacheke waved her hand, "No, my child!"

"That is my position."

"No, I said!"

"Yes!" Emphatically, he replied to her.

"Then take her for a second wife if you must, my child."

"Nooo!" he screamed at her.

"How can you be so impudently adamant?" his father bawled, bursting forth and cutting him with a slap across the face. Mutende bent, fresh blood steaming in his nostrils. He exhaled in his palm and what he saw was terrifying. His muscles began to cringe, contorting with adrenaline. "Take her, undress your Betty and do on her what Mutende has refused to perform."

And his father leapt like a cat, slitting his face with another slap, causing a momentary lifting of Mutende's torso. Sweat and tears and mucus mingled in one face.

"Why do you cry for a grandchild as if you were an impotent father of impotent sons? Give my loins the chance yours were given!" Mutende was in a frenzy.

"*Woowe*, we are dead!" Namacheke wailed, confronting

the son!! "How could you? Do you want me to show you your real mother? Do you want to peer into the nakedness that bared itself beneath your father for your own coming? Or is it these breasts that you and your five brothers shriveled that you want to set your tongue against?" she said, undoing her bra in a frenzy.

"No, no! Namacheke, do not be blinded by rage. You are a mother. Do not do such a thing to ruin your own child!" Odinga's wife implored.

"How can a child I killed myself to bear say the things he has said to his father?" Namacheke screamed fighting of those restraining her.

"Leave me! I say leave me. Today he will see me the way I arrived from my mother's womb, or I am not Namacheke, the grand daughter of Siambi-Malakha, his great grandfather who made a leopard cry in his arms."

"Let her do it. Let her show me everything. Let Namacheke unfold those papyrus buttocks and a son will lash them for a mother!" Mutende was now fighting back frantically. Seeing this, Namacheke charged, kicking away those riveted on her. Then she started loosening the knots of her dress. By the time another hand tried to reach her again, she was through with the dress. It collapsed, rimming her feet in an uneven heap. Her fingers then frenziedly linked to a black petticoat, broke the strap and started scratching through the gullies of her tummy to set free the remaining attachments. There was evidence that the petticoat was on its way, and Odinga's wife cast herself upon Namacheke.

111

"Let her do it. If I die, I die!" Mutende advanced.

"You are mad! There is something in your head, you boy!" Odinga shouted, charging; Mafulu close at heel. They were all approaching him. And suddenly Mutende mustered feats of energy. He turned, and twined and twirled. But the hands on his shoulders dug in the more. Then Mutende noticed his legs were free and so he used them: there was a stampede of feet altering, rumbling under the sudden shift of weight. Odinga, safe by an instinctive dive, was plastered where he had taken cover. Everybody was scattered like grain in a drying yard. But his father lay across the torso of his mother in a slanting crouch, clutching his belated manhood; grunting in raw agony. Mutende's kick had reached a lethal depth. Mutende turned himself violently; shaking off the hands riveted on him. And next he was fighting with nothing; there were no more hands, no more voices. They had melted; His father's grunt gone in the sudden silence. The wind outside began to blow hard.

And suddenly, a shrill cry grew rending the silence. Mutende turned from his bed waking up with a start. His arm was hanging loosely on the side of the bedstead and it was aching. Mutende was wet, sweating, shaking.

The baby was still crying. For more than a week, the baby had been crying. The elders said it was because of tummy *snakes*. The baby was still crying. That cry pierced his ears. The noise cut through his heart tearing through his left ear, drilling into the right and churning before bursting out. A thick feeling burnt its way down the vent of his throat. Then it congealed and clogged the inside. It was like a hot potato. He closed his tearing eyes and made an effort to swallow. It could not go. It stayed there. Mutende could hardly breathe. He struggled for balance, onto his knees: choking.

"Husband! Help and bring some water for the baby," Betty said in shaking voice.

"Whose husband? You have no husband in me, do you hear?" he spat out.

"O, do not talk like that. Do we have to go through this every day? Let us not go back, please!"

"Back to what? I do not like you and I hate you. Get out of my life, woman."

"I am your wife –," she was barely pleading.

"Not my wife. And I do not love you," he cried.

"But you are my husband," she pleaded.

"No! You do not love me. You want to dump yourself on me. But it is Rose I love. It is only Rose that I want," he was getting hysterical.

"I love you, Mutende. If you can give me a chance, I will make a good wife and a mother –"

"I can't, and I want you out of my life," he pushed her. She staggered, missing the baby by inches.

"Mutende, what if I fell onto the baby? We are also people," she reiterated sharply.

"Then go away. Go away with your child."

"Where do you expect us to go?"

"Did I call you here?" he moved towards where her voice was coming from.

"Why then do you want me to go away when you did not invite me here? You can get a rope and pull us out if you wish. But I came here to marry. After all it won't be the first relationship with a problem." Hearing this, he jumped towards the voice, got her by the waist and attempted to pull her out. She clung to the central pole in the hut, holding it tight.

"This is my home as much as you are my husband, the father of my child."

"You will never be my wife. I swear, upon my dead body."

"Then leave me alone," she said, pushing him off hard and leaping back to regain her hold on the pole for support.

"My god!" he screamed as he hit his head against the wall.

"Sorry, my husband, I did not mean to hurt —" she said, hurrying towards where the sound of the fall came from. He had bolted out. The tail of her voice was lost behind him. His eyes could not see. His ears could not hear. Mutende was boiling with rage. This was the limit. He had to go and face his parents once and for all. He had to tell them his mind and then leave them for good. He would never marry her.

All he knew was that his parents' house was somewhere. Ahead.

What seemed like the first stride had sailed him halfway across the courtyard. His feet made contact with what sounded like a bench and Mutende staggered onto all fours, straightened and still wobbled on. He did not even notice his brother who was clearing the drinking place put back the fallen bench. The other four brothers opened the doors of their houses and looked and saw a brother stagger away from the bench and the bang the contact had caused. As he neared the parents' bedroom, Mutende's pace steadied, slowing towards the entrance.

The door was half-open. The candle was still burning. His hand moved to knock but hesitated. The message was just to be as simple and straight as, "It is all over!" And that he was parting to nurture his own sperm; bound by blood.

He stepped forward again. The bedroom was as quiet as a tomb.

His eye, through the hinges of the door, saw something move; something like a shadow. Then it was all still again. Then another shadow moved but this one was darker and it seemed shorter. Or was it still the same shadow?

Then he heard the sound of a hand-broom inside the bedroom. It was moving at a casual pace. As if on the same spot. His mother was sweeping. Sweeping at this hour?

Then a voice. He heard one. It was stealthy; it was low. Then laughter; small and deep. From inside the bedroom. Mutende made another step: a shorter one this time. Then he slightly edged his head in.

A body of a man was sprawled on the floor. It was stretched on a mat at the foot of a neatly laid bed, his parents' bed. The body was alive, its gaze planted on the apex of the roof. Half of it was covered. Then the hands of the man moved. Then the whole of the man moved. Just a bit. The person was not steady. He was drunk. It was his father Mafulu. Mafulu's hand then wound towards a bottle next to him and emptied its contents down the throat. It was a bottle of *changa* liquor Mutende's father had drunk. He slumped back and he did not move again. The bottle rolled towards the head of the bed and knocked the foot of a table. Mutende pushed his head another point through the doorway and he heard his own voice ahead of him, "Mama!"

A broom moved fast.

A black out!

"What is it my child?" and his mother exclaimed, "Grandmother in the spirit world, the candle has lost its flame!" But in the moment between light, the hand and the darkness, a shadow had moved. The shadow had moved again! Mutende was sure this was a thief. A thief had sneaked into the house, into the parents' bedroom and hidden behind the darkness. Mutende had to move now. His feet grazed his father's body. The edge of a table turned and something that sounded like a laden table capsized. His hand searched the darkness for the shadow and he felt a figure and his hands dug in and held firm.

"A thief!" Mutende's voice carried his cry into the still night, his grip gaining on the limp body, dragging it into the courtyard.

Five doors slammed, their occupants converging in, from the perimeter of his brothers' huts all armed with their torches. The first torch flashed and lit the limp figure.

It was Odinga's face. It was Odinga in Mutende's hands.

So Odinga was the thief. So this thief was the Odinga who had denied me my love, imposed on me a stranger and a child and now he had sneaked into my father's bedroom to steal! So many things were flashing in Mutende's mind.

Before any word could emerge from Odinga's sagged mouth, Mutende had leapt like a cheetah and was already returning from his hut, his elbow angled and before his elder brother could hold a hand back, a glistening knife had cut into, come out and dug back and into Odinga. Odinga's hands clutched around this thrust into his navel, holding the knife, his face twisted with pain. Odinga's muscles then wilted into a fading frown and his body started sagging.

Namacheke, horrified by the son's swift hand, which she had seen through the window of her bedroom, had fallen upon her husband, shrieking, before passing out. Mafulu had staggered on to his fours and glared at the hour of his revelation and groped for light.

And from inside the parents' house, a hinge turned and to the outside, a dim candle approached. Heavy feet slouched in from the darkness, feet empty of life. Mafulu's hand raised the candle upwards, towards the face of the wilting man. The sons, with bare chests, stood awed. Mafulu's hand was trembling, as the light slowly returned down the length of Odinga's naked body that lay on its back in the grass. Mafulu's quivering hand touched crouched fingers of the body, still holding on the sword of his undoing. The hands of the body then sank to the sides leaving a fresh knife-deep inside. The knife seemed an extrusion of a banana shoot out of damp earth. Mafulu's unstable hand pulled out the knife, long and now crimson and wet. It left behind a deep hole in the tummy and there, around the navel was a white mark curving a circumference around it.

Mafulu's eyes turned away from the haunting sign. He stared ahead into the circle of sons surrounding him and their body; the body of his matrimonial anchor. A tear of thick blood trickled out. Mutende clutched onto his navel as if in attempt to stop blood from pouring out of the fallen man's navel. And as if by inherent motion all the sons looked at each other and in unison their eyes pooled down onto the navel of their fallen father. Staring through the dying light of the candle, the distinct birthmark radiated, replicating itself on the orbit of the navels, of all the six half-naked sons that stood around it. And another tear of blood pushed out as if by some deep contraction, another followed and suddenly a stream started flowing, drenching the birthmark, and inundating it in its blood. The candle fell out of Mafulu's hand. It tilted to the side but it did not die out; it continued to glow. Mafulu rose with the knife in his hands, at a growing angle, he turned slowly and a silhouette filtered into the darkness. Mutende watched the fallen shoulders of Mafulu fade into the night. Odinga's face relaxed and his head fell to the side in a peaceful slump and Mutende's knees gave way.

"No!" He fell onto his father's body, burying his head in the cold blood of his father. Why? Father, why? Why did you keep away this truth? Why did they make and keep this infertile lie. Did Mafulu have to borrow? Father did you have to lend your blood? So you let us live a lie, you let the flesh be ploughed into itself. O this blood of secrecy!" Mutende lifted his head; his nose clogged his face thick with shivering clots. His bothers did not notice his red eyes; each lost in their darkness. Mutende shook his father. "Father of my Rose, Rose of my love, Rose of my incest. O' this darkness of Mutende. This darkness of my undoing. Did you have to do this?" he cried, staggering in the opposite direction, away from all.

Behind him, a baby's voice followed him, cutting into the night. And Mutende wobbled away; into the other darkness.

The Muzungu's Pupu

We had never seen anything like this before. At least not in our family. Then it just happened one day. Just like that. Mother had been taken away from us while we were asleep and he promised she would be returned. I was there when father promised the four of us. It was now running into the second day and we were still sitting with our eyes scanning the doorway. It was as if mother was travelling from Mars on foot. And then she suddenly appeared through the door. I remember us scrambling for vantage positions like little puppies along the udder of an exhausted mother.

Unlike mother dog's parade of breasts, it was a little bundle that mother delicately held across her arms that took our breaths away. We had never seen anything with such a skin before. Not in our house. When we did, it was only once a week. Once a week and on Sundays. We saw it at the Catholic mission when our parents went with us for mass. It's only father Mesmeris who looked like that. People rarely called Fr. Mesmeris by his name. They just called him Muzungu. Muzungu was a Kiswahili word with variations such as *omusungu*, *omuzungu*, *mujungu* and *emusugut* depending on the part of the country you were hearing it from. Translated into English, this meant White person.

"Is this one omusungu?" Nyongesa asked with a gaping mouth. Mother smiled and replied, "Your sister is!"

"Omusungu, omusungu!" we started chanting,

leaping and circling the furniture. And before long, one of us was limping. Then we heard her voice for the first time. "She is hungry," mother explained as we scrambled, applying on each other elbows and pressured heels to maintain closer view. Mother brought out a breast that dripped like it had a little shy puncture. The baby's mouth moved blindly like that of a bat and mother plugged the nipple in its mouth.

It pulled at the breast.

"Eh eh!" Nyongesa exclaimed then looked at me. There was a light in his eyes. I looked at him in wonder and we laughed in a symphony of choreographed echoes. Kaloli looked at us, removed his thumb from his mouth and also joined our duet but rather on a higher note then threw his head back with more freedom but rather too fast. A rescue dive from our bigger brother who was all along trying to act like a man came but a fraction late; Kaloli's head had contacted the ground and his mouth opened like a trumpet, completely out of tune. The baby also started crying.

Mother said, "If you do not stop crying, Satan will hear you and come for the baby," and Kaloli just stopped like a bulb that had been switched off.

The following day we were still squatting around the *karaya* – the metallic basin – as they washed our Omusungu.

"Eh eh! Mama what is this?" Nyongesa asked.

Mother deflected his hand and explained, "She is a girl."

"Mama! Look, omusungu does not have *koko!*" I shouted and looked at Nyongesa with an open mouth.

"God created her like that," she explained, applying another lather of *Johnson's* baby soap.

"Why?" I asked.

"Because girls are special people. Girls are angels," she smiled, looking up at me.

"A girl, a girl!" Nyongesa began another chant. I soon joined him on some kind of vertical dance.

Then I soon realised that Kaloli had cheated me. He had moved to the left hand side of mother where baby's head was. And a better position to see the face of Omusungu pulling at mum's breast. I tried to pluck him away. He reached for a hold on baby's shawl and mother's hand curved a quick umbrella over the baby's face. "Obote!" she warned me.

"But that is my place," I insisted.

"But did God create that place for you?" Big bro asked. Although a storyteller who was always the hero in his many folktales, big bro was always trying to act like Dad whenever father set foot out of the house.

"But I was the one who was here first?" My voice quivered with a silver of tears lining my eyes.

"Obote, one of these days you are going to kill a person in this home," mother warned, powdering the baby.

"And father will cut off those ears and give them to a hyena," Nyongesa reminded me.

"Enough of that Nyongesa!" mother wound him down.

"Obote, there is still space, enough space for you and the whole clan. Eh, and stop rubbing your eyes like that. If you continue like that I will take Omusungu back."

"Back?" I let drop my hands and raised a quizzical face.

"Back to the doctor," Mother looked serious.

"But they say God is the one who gives babies," Nyongesa said.

"Mother, mother, motheeeeer! And where do babies come from?" I asked tagging mother's skirt for attention.

Then I saw big brother rising and strutting towards the kitchen with an artificial frown on his forehead.

"Babies?" mother continued. "You go to hospital and while you are asleep the angels of God bring the baby and lay it in the arms of the doctor. And when you wake up the doctor gives you the baby."

"And the angels take away your pillow!" I wondered.

"O, you mean the pillow on the stomach?" I nodded to her question. "The doctor gets it out when you are asleep and makes a little mattress for baby," mother answered with a smile, laying the baby on her little mattress in the cradle, covering her tenderly and rolling over a mosquito net. Mother then gave each of us a segment of sugar cane and told us to watch over Muzungu's sleep.

The baby's voice cut through the silent bedroom atmosphere and mother burst in, the comb that was hanging from her wild hair falling behind her as she made for the baby's cot.

"Mother, Mother, it is Obote." Nyongesa was trying to shout above Kaloli's voice. My gamble to impress the baby with sugar cane had not worked out. When they confiscated my cane, it was not only the loss of it or Nyongesa's taunting laughter that disturbed me; it was Kaloli's reporting me to Mother that I was planning to beg for a piece of his cane, which caused much concern.

"Children who begin begging end up picking things that do not belong to them," mother reminded me as she dressed up to go to the women's club. I did not want to be a thief. For Dad had told us that many of those half-naked convicts he watched over were seasoned thieves, some of who started in a simple way, picking ordinary things like chicken eggs and cold food from their mother's pots. "Some of those you see slashing there and lifting those heavy buckets from the public toilets began with sifting through their father's pockets and ended up making off with people's bulls," father had often scared more than cautioned us.

But I loved sugar cane as Kaloli did Colgate. Mother knew that her son loved sugar cane and I prayed that this knowledge would move a mother's heart. But it was not like it was about to happen. I then shifted my hope, that Nyongesa would soon consider me with understanding as he sat strategically in front of me, fingering his piece of cane with interested eyes. Then Nyongesa gave his cane a sweeping bite and with an angled head started chewing his it loudly like a dog slurping water.

"Nyongesa, is that how people eat?" mother turned to him.

"No, mother," he said apologetically, in a loud voice and then turned towards me in a stealthy voice and added, "Aha, but sugar cane is very sweet!" he said this showing me a got-you-this-time kind of eye.

"And keep an eye on the baby. If it starts crying there is milk in the bottle," mother called out to Taaka the maid, straightening and setting her headscarf.

"And if it takes milk and then cries?" Nyongesa asked, between a chewing mouth.

"I am at the club," mother said, making a knot on her headdress before getting out through the main door.

Nyongesa looked at me, paused and then made a loud bite that sounded like one snapping a cane with a knee and a stream of juice flowed down his mouth wetting his stomach. I swallowed saliva and waited. He looked at me and then placed the cane down carefully like a piece of glass. Then he got up and marched into the kitchen, his right eye over the shoulder just in case I attempted 'something silly.' With him now far, his sugar cane appeared very close to me. But I knew what he was spoiling for.

I knew a fight with him was like picking up soldier ants with your tongue. I was not about to register a first victory. Nyongesa returned with a *gama* (mug) of water and resumed his place on the floor before picking the cane. He then looked it over, as if to ascertain that I had not touched it, before giving it a bite that must have been heard next door. So he would crunch the cane, swallow the juice and then escort it down with a mouthful of water and then he would go back to the cane and then to the water.

Soon he set such a rhythm that Kaloli kept laughing at those intervals. Kaloli laughed louder each time Nyongesa made the from-cane-to-water cycle.

"Why are you laughing?" I looked at him.

"Touch me, I will cry until father comes back," Kaloli warned me.

Named after my father's father in-law Kaloli was a darling to our Dad. You only touched Kaloli if you were ready for the consequences. That aside, it was not so much the threat of having our ears chopped by father that worried me as the prospect of Kaloli crying until the chicken returned.

This small in-law of my father could cry, empty his voice and just keep the cry going with some beetle-like sound, fall asleep, wake up two hours later, remember where he stopped and then just continue from where he ended. His favourite position was the veranda next to the door where father had to pass when returning home. So the humming bird would continue. Once he started crying you would hear nothing else except the little fellow's voice in erratic disregard of tonality. Then you'd pray for father to come in, hand you your share for disturbing his father-in-law and have some peace, for that was the only way to switch off the *beetle*. So I was not going to begin what I could not stop.

"You have refused to give me some of your sugar cane?" I implored more than asked.

Instead of replying with words, Nyongesa bit another crunch and juice flowed watering his tummy. Kaloli laughed. Nyongesa looked at me, crooked his finger, wound it over his tummy and gave it a popping lick. Kaloli again laughed until he fell on his little back.

"Okay, you will see!" I said losing hope.

"What will you do?" Nyongesa said in a what-can-you-also-do-after-all tone.

"I am going to the toilet and I will stay there forever and you will not come in," I said, edging towards the loo.

"Coming in for what?" he replied in a voice like he had never seen the inside of a toilet since he was born.

"Where are you going to urinate?" I sounded like the bigger stronger brother.

"Who tells you I urinate?" he challenged me.

"Liar, when yesterday I saw you doing it."

"Doing what?" he said sneeringly.

"Urinating. You removed your pair of shorts and put them down here," I touched the spot on the floor. "I saw you and then you went inside. I heard you urinating *chorrrrr!* Yes, you urinate." It was like I was ready to go to court to prove it. I had evidence.

"Okay, that was yesterday. I am now a cowboy. I won't urinate again," he said in a triumphant way.

But from the way his eyes were darting I knew he was about to do something snappy. And had I not made a leap onto the toilet seat, he would have reached it a second ahead of me. I secured the seat with both hands riveted to the sides, spreading out my little bottom far to avoid sagging in the tray. I turned and taunted him with a face of a prince on some contested throne.

"Close the door." Nyongesa warned, but more in disappointment.

"I will not." And I meant it.

"But you are in the toilet. So close the door," he sounded determined.

"Me, I want to see outside." My voice must have told him my degree of determination. Nyongesa paused. From the way he was fidgeting with his fly, the *Gamas* of water he had gulped were certainly on their way out. So I turned to give my hands a firmer hold on the toilet seat and spread myself over like an octopus. And when I looked up Nyongesa had disappeared like roast meat in a dream, you bend to wash your hands to sit up and find it has vanished.

"Obote!" I heard his voice calling me but I did not answer. There was a pause. "What is this?" his tone was friendly and inviting this time.

"What?" I asked.

"Come and see it," he invited me but still out of view.

"Bring it here."

"I have found your sugar cane and you want me to bring it?" There was a pause, and then he said, "Mother kept it here." He sounded so excited but much closer.

"Where?"

"This way." He sounded like he was over my shoulder.

"You are deceiving me?"

"Okay let me eat it then you will know —"

It was like he had catapulted a stone from a sling. Off the seat, I stumbled forward, trapped by my shorts, my bum popping out of the pants. I separated from the shorts and strutted forward freely like an ant without wings.

But I could not see Nyongesa. He had disappeared like a ghost. "Nyongesa! Nyongesa! Where-?" I stopped. Something was chuckling behind me and when I spun it was Nyongesa, comfortable on the toilet seat. And from the way his eyes moved, his knotted lips and eyeballs frozen in action, this was not a time to attempt a scuffle. It would be a dirty one. Then I heard someone snort and saw big brother enter, led by his nose, "Mh, Nyongesa! With the door open, how can you?" Big Bro plugged two fingers in his nose, slammed the toilet door and rushed out gasping for fresher air.

And where was Kaloli? I wondered. I peeped and I saw him by the sewing machine fidgeting with its contents. I then saw his little hand push back the bobbin drawer before trotting to the baby's cot. There was no body seeing me and so I gently pushed behind me the door leading to the bedroom.

"What it is it, what is it?" Nyongesa burst out of the toilet. By now Kaloli was wriggling on the ground like two male snakes wrestling over something.

"Taaka! Taaka!" he screamed hopping to the kitchen!

The maid leapt in through the kitchen door and rammed her chest into his head through the doorway and sending him staggering in reverse before rushing back to the toilet to affix his pants. Kaloli's mouth was dripping yellow. All yellow like he had attempted to drink the fresh yolk of an egg!

"What has happened?" Taaka asked anxious like one treating snakebite.

"It's Obote. He gave him something!" Nyongesa explained

Although Kaloli was gifted in pitch, I had never heard a human being of his size hit such upper notes. Honestly I was dead. I was dead. God, I had not intended to.

"Obote, what did you give Kaloli?" Taaka was wiping her nose with the hem of her dress, her eyes now red like the flower outside our house. Not a word came out of my mouth. I was just staring in the doorway. Father was going to cut off my ears and give them to a hyena for real. For sure, a soldier is more likely to keep his promise than recycle it.

At this time it was like Kaloli's eyes were on their way out. He rammed his little fist into the cup of water Taaka was trying to hold to his mouth. The metallic cup spun, rolled and hit the baby's basin. Metal met metal, there was a big bang and that woke up the baby with a loud cry. Taaka was running between the 'two babies' and reaching none.

"Nyongesa, run to the club," she said, lifting her dress to her nose exposing loose cotton pants and a navel the size of a mushroom.

"It was Obote who gave him something," Taaka tried to exonerate herself.

"What?" Mother was animated.

"Obote is here!" Nyongesa tried to have his finger

on my head but he crossed paths with mother, the sole of mother's shoe grazed his toe "aya yah!" he screamed and went hopping to the nearest chair!

Kaloli's tongue was now hanging out like the ears of an elephant. It was now light-yellow like he had eaten *omutalo*, the first milk from a lactating cow.

"Someone's child is dying. What will I tell him? I am dead," mother exclaimed raising her hands to the back of her head.

"Mama, it is Obote," Nyongesa continued before bending to resume fanning his toes with his breath.

"Where will I tell him I had gone when this happened? Taaka what did he give the child?" mother asked more out of desperation that in search of an answer.

"I was in the kitchen." But as she pleaded, it was like mother not listening to her.

"Baba, what did he give you my child?" she was now scrubbing Kaloli's tongue with a tablecloth.

"Obote," Kaloli pointed at me, "gave me omusungu's pupu."

Mother straightened and went still, like one listening to a night sound. Then she bent low. "He gave you baby's pupu! How could he? And you, Taaka –"

"Mother, I was in the – "Taaka tried to plead.

"Stop singing about the kitchen … and you, child, I have told you this before, that one day you will kill a person," mother said, approaching the corner where I was holed. But before she spread her hand to do a horizontal swipe, Kaloli's voice rang out sharp and fresh like a metal workshop. Mother whirled and leaped to where he was wriggling from. "And where were you also?" she cast her hands desperately at Taaka before, shoving her aside and lifting Kaloli by the feet to the sink and dangling him over a few unwashed plates before switching him down. "Get me the *karaya* quickly," she screamed at Taaka. And rising, she cupped water bending down to throw the handfuls into Kaloli's mouth while angling him over the basin, her body moving like an archaic wooden hand pump.

Then she stopped with a start and looked at the boy quizzically "Kaloli, where are you spitting the water?"

"Mother, he has been swallowing it," Nyongesa added.

"*Woweee*, I am dead! The child has swallowed all the pupu," she exclaimed.

With the swiftness of a butcher's hand she hung him upside down like a dead rat and Kaloli puked out a lump of yellow before being switched upright to avoid choking. Then he started retching.

"Call your father quickly," mother signalled my big bro who'd just come in. Her tears were rolling faster than those of Kaloli and Taaka. Nyongesa looked closer at mothers face and out of nowhere her burst into a wail.

"Taaka, that baby will start bleeding in the navel, if it continues crying like that; you can see what I am still doing. Give it gripe water! Nyongesa, stop crying like that and bring my money purse. Thank you for being a good boy, my son," she said, opening the purse. "Now run to the road and stop any vehicle you see going up the road." And

Nyongesa shot out like a thief. Mother closed the purse and pushed it into her left bra where she always kept her money when going out to the shops. She turned to Kaloli, wiping his tummy, "My god, what will I tell the man happened to his child?"

Father stepped one foot in the doorway, and next he was craning up Kaloli in his arms. "Where were you when this happened?" he demanded, eyes straight in mother's face.

"Let's take him to hospital," she pleaded.

"It's Obote," Nyongesa entered, panting.

"My God, he is all yellow. Or is it yellow fever!" Father sounded confused.

"This one is the one who gave him yellow pupu," Nyongesa said, touching my head. Father narrowed his eyes

"You must be joking?" Father straightened himself and faced mother.

"Please, let's take the child to hospital first. It could be a fever," mother's voice was holding on a thread.

"And then say what? And the people start saying 'there goes the sergeant whose son gave his son *pupu*.'" and he clicked. "As far as I can remember, no child in the history of our clan has ever attempted anything near this."

"So what are you suggesting?" mother said in a tone I had never heard her talk back to father. She then made two strides to my corner. "Look at this!" she said, stretching out my ear right above my head.

"What about them?" father was visibly upset.

133

"We don't have this in our line," she said releasing my ear and letting it flap back. Then she mumbled something about my grandmother having tainted her children with wide ears.

"You have never had any respect for my mother." Father's tone was high. He sounded as if my mother had slapped his mother.

"*Aya, Mama mama,*" Kaloli started kicking. He always did this whenever attention was being shifted from him.

"*Bas bas!*" Father struggled to calm him.

The baby also started crying.

"Taaka!" Mother called wiping red eyeballs "bring that Josephine here."

"*Muko!*" Father lifted Kaloli. Muko was the endeared form for a male in-law and that is how father usually referred to Kaloli as *Muko*. "Now tell me exactly, what did you eat?"

"It is Obote. He gave me Omusungu's pupu," he said, slumping his mouth on father's chest. Father creased his nose avoiding Kaloli's face before lowering him to the ground delicately like a water pot.

"Are you sure he gave him pupu?" father had another frown on the face.

"You have heard it with your ears!" mother answered.

"Here!" father passed Kaloli's hand to mother.

"What again?" mother wondered.

"Smell his mouth.... we have to establish, if it is real pupu!"

"But am I the only one with a nose here?" mother's voice was on the edge of tears.

Father hesitated and then said, as if commanding a parade. "I have a cold!"

"*Ii,* did the flu wait for this to happen –"

"Woman, do you know that I have just sneaked out without permission. I am on duty officially. You are wasting government time, if you must be reminded." From the way his eyes bulged, I thought Taaka was wise to take the baby from mother, freeing her hands. Mother then took Kaloli and held him close. She lowered her face to Kaloli's who in turn rolled out half of his tongue.

"Put that tongue back." Mother's tone was high. "Kaloli, did you hear me? Now if you refuse, a fly is going to fall on it and –" Kaloli stacked it back reluctantly, but left the mouth open enough for any wandering fly. Mother flapped the lips together like the lid of a teapot and pressed them as if she was going to secure it with a lock. She then edged her nose forward in cautious instalments. Then she stopped and looked at father as if she was listening, as if she was wondering.

Father listened anxiously, and then edged forward. "Is it the thing?"

She shook her head.

"Then what is it?" Father's face was more puzzled. "You know what? Smell again."

"What?" mother sounded like she was crying any minute.

"Smell that mouth but more closely this time," father said in a friendly tone.

"You know, a baby's pupu does not smell, particularly in the first days." He added.

"It does. It smells," ,other assured him.

"Like what?" Father's face was between doubt and surprise.

"Like scrambled egg." It was like mother wanted to laugh after saying this. "So, try to smell it for me," mother turned Kaloli to father.

"Why?" father asked taking a step back.

"You know we women do not eat chicken or even eggs. But you eat them. Smell for me!" mother said.

"But who cooks the eggs. Who serves those eggs? So find out that smell. NOW!" Father sounded like he had blown a whistle or commanded 'attention', like he would not add another word, but only action, after that.

Then for the first time, father turned and looked at me. I was bundled in the corner of the room hardly visible except for my yam-leaf ears sticking out. This was the end, I knew. What began as my first offer to my little sister had brought me face to face with father's anger. He always warned against fighting. Now that I had not only done what I did but also actually touched his little father in-law, he was going to do the one thing he had promised; 'cut off my ears.'

"Obote, what did you give your brother?" he asked without raising his voice. But I did not hear a word; *I just saw his mouth open and then close without a word and then his eyes bulging out like those of a swine being roasted whole.*

"Obote, am I talking to a stone?" But instead I heard. *"Are all those ears for decoration?"*

"Tell me what you gave him and I will not punish you?" My ears heard, *"I have always promised to cut of those winnowers which you pass for ears. So today-?"* My pants felt warm and a little stream flowed towards the door.

"Are you going to tell me?" And I heard, *"and then I will give them to Karimojong warriors to take to hyenas"."*

"Obote!" There was now a rusty edge to his voice. *Then I closed my eyes and saw a wide knife rise splitting the air below as it fell towards me.* I held onto my ears, knitted my eyelids and I screamed. Kaloli, the baby, all went silent.

Father then sighed, frowned and turned to my mother. She was bent over the chair putting back the baby's nappy.

"I cannot see any pupu, not even in the bed," she said. Father then looked at Kaloli. His little T-shirt that mother had just dressed him in for hospital was yellow, with more Saliva still lining out of his mouth. The tongue hung out of the mouth like a goat's placenta. There were cakes of yellow on the edges of his mouth. He lifted up Kaloli, his little frame fitting in his hands. "Muko, if a fly falls on the tongue it will not fit in your mouth again" and Kaloli replaced the tongue back and it fitted.

Father went with him perched on the shoulder. He bent as they went under the doorframe into the bathroom and returned with Kaloli's delicacy, a tube of Colgate toothpaste. He held the other end of it and let his *muko* suck as much out of the tube as he could squeeze. He gave him a second and a third, allowing Kaloli to milk the tube halfway.

"Now *muko,* tell me, where did he get the musungu's pupu?"

Kaloli's little finger pointed ahead. Father got Kaloli's other hand into his and followed his son of about two years through one door into another room. From behind the chair, where I was crumpled; I saw them stop by the sewing machine. "Here!" he said, standing in his toes and pointing his finger above his head and when father opened the bobbin drawer, he found one quinine tablet remaining.

Napunyi

The village of Masyaka stretched on either side of a valley and in it lived common folk as in any African village. They were simple people who farmed their land for a livelihood. Here women woke up to a rope of responsibilities and slept with one eye open waiting for the horizon to ripen and bear another day, another day for men to dictate instructions in the morning, and return at dawn, from drink and elsewhere, to catch some sleep. But there were also women who talked about people and others who smoked. There was such a one who gossiped and smoked like a kitchen. Napunyi was her name. Some said Napunyi was good because she helped people know what was happening in the village, others said she was bad because she spilt people's secrets. Such folks would exclaim and say, "Napunyi is Napunyi." Others would just slap their palms and sigh, "Ah, whatever is on Napunyi has mother and child!"

And people were not really bothered that she talked like a jingle bell or that she was as lazy as *Khayindikiri*, the little bird who always complained of a broken wing whenever she was asked to work but would be quick to join those at table saying "*nekekere nekekere* eating in no work." For many stole a word on their way to the well, by beer pots, while gathering firewood and also in the markets. For then the village came to know whose husband serves sauce when it's chicken but remembers that men should not peer into pots when vegetables are cooked; the husband who crawled from drink and could not differentiate between the needy parts of his wife and her armpit; the youth who went under his girlfriend and got his foreskin harvested, and also the woman whose children keep connecting from door to door, trailing the aroma of roast meat. This gossip was sweet like morning sleep. It lifted the heart. It did not kill.

But Napunyi's gossiping was of another kind.

For once she opened her mouth, many would stare with tearful eyes while others would cup their heads in their palms and wonder, "What kind of woman is this?"

Napunyi had a husband and they called him Okomba. Often Okomba and Napunyi would disagree on her gossiping and her addiction to smoking.

"What kind of person are you who will never settle unless you hold a cigarette?" Okomba said on this particular day as he tussled with her over a basket of flour that she had stashed to go and barter for cigarettes.

"Okomba, did I stop you from smoking or do you want me to steal from someone else's garden in order to get myself a stick to smoke?" she snarled, fighting back, overpowering him and wringing the basket out of his smarting hands. Okomba made another attempt to reach this only remaining food in the house but a whole day's hunger undermined his leap.

"You can take the whole of it. Let us starve and die. You can go and uproot all from the garden and smoke it. But I tell you Napunyi, what will kill you will come through a cigarette," he cursed.

The truth is that Napunyi had not smoked for two days and all she needed was a cigarette or she would just *die*. And cigarettes had become scarce. But just last evening, she had heard that a neighbour had smuggled in a few from Kenya and so Napunyi had told herself, "if only I could stock at least a packet for myself, that would see me through the uncertain days ahead. I must get the cigarettes!" Not even a crane would hold her back.

She turned and saw Okomba eyeing her; his face looking like a mask, sprayed by the flour as they struggled. His lower mouth twitched, his eyes narrowed behind the contorting mask of white, and Napunyi knew he was really on edge. She hesitated, scooped two bowls of flour for the day's supper, swung the basket onto her head and just walked out. Okomba saw her shadow disappear past the feet of her son, Abangi. Abangi was leaning against the wall of the house staring in the feathers of a little bird he had trapped for his supper: a dog had leapt away with it.

"You boy, why don't you pick a pail and go to the well, or won't your mother need water to cook your supper?" Okomba barked at the boy. Abangi just clicked, and looked in the direction the dog had vanished.

"You boy!" Okomba warned.

"Don't I have a name for you to call me 'boy' or do you think I am your house boy to go and fetch water for you! You can go and cook with your saliva!" The boy said and strutted away. Like always. And Okomba swore to himself; I will not see the headmaster of the village school for his enrolment. Unless I am not Okomba himself!"

Abangi had never gone through a classroom door. Some children even laughed at him singing about how he was the village goat that could not name the colour of a blackboard. What he would do, as if in retaliation, was to waylay them on their way to school; at times relieving them of the dry pieces of cassava which they would be taking to class for use as chalk. With a mug, he strapped with a banana fibre on his waist, he'd slope to the well, scoop a quantity of water and make himself a light breakfast. Abangi would also go hunting birds and picking mushrooms when the season came. He did not go to school not because fees were impossible to come by, after all there were those who could manage to send their children to school at least one term in a year or barter their labour for fees, but because Napunyi preferred spending on cigarettes to everything else.

This boy has never recognized me as his father or even as a somebody, however much I try, Okomba thought. Those who try to tame the guinea fowl should always remember it is a bird, he reminded himself mopping the smarting hands he had been cooling with a wet rag, Okomba turned restlessly boiling with anger over what he saw as Abangi's impudence. He swore he had had enough of Napunyi and her child. He stared ahead into the milky horizon over the sappy hedge that stood between his homestead and that of Opyema, his neighbour. A pang of hunger cut his inside. Okomba swallowed a dry throat and mumbled something like "Let me also ignore them and see if I will die. The thankless goats! I won't do any more work for them. And I mean it. Unless I am not Okomba himself."

He leaned back on the wall and closed his eyes and thought: what a lazy wife of a woman!

On top of being lazy and calculating, Napunyi also drove her husband like a donkey. And women pitied him. Not because all of them treated their husbands like angels but because Okomba was unlike many husbands: he never returned home at dawn because he never drank. He never drank because he had one leg. He had one leg because his stepmother had cut the other one off. She cut it off because her husband had threatened to divorce her if she did not bear him a baby boy. And so she had seen a medicine man that had asked for the leg of her husband's only son. And when she had taken it, the medicine man had said it was the wrong leg and when she was about to take away the right one, her husband had found her and she was buried the next day.

And since then Okomba had lived with one leg and the women said a mother should not have done that. And they showed him kindness, sympathy and heart like the missionary who saw him hop, falter and fall, thirty years ago, as he knelt for Holy Communion and sent him a wooden leg that had now become a part of him.

Okomba opened his eyes and stretched his left leg that was getting numb as a result of supporting more of his weight on it. He sighed. He was really getting hungrier. He knew one truth; that despite swearing that he would not labour for Napunyi and her ingrate son, he'd need to eat. Okomba was hungry; very hungry. He knew that after all the foul words they spat in each other's face they would want something to eat, water to bathe and cook; like always. So Okomba had said, "but this is the last time I am doing it. Unless I am not Okomba himself." Affixing his limb and reaching for the water container, he began his journey down to the well.

Apart from women and children, Okomba was the only man, in the village who went to the well. When Okomba picked his tin and stomped his wooden limb down the valley to the springs of Masyaka, children would follow and women pause, gazing at Okomba do his thing: swinging the metallic *edebe* into the air and letting it settle onto his head like a dove on her nest. And not a single drop of water would spill to the ground. And people would say;

"If only he had been created a woman, he could have made a wonderful wife!"

So as Okomba returned, trudging up the hill with his tin of water, praying and hoping that Napunyi had returned to prepare the family a meal, he passed two old women plucking the bark of a mango tree for medicinal purposes. They looked at him and one with a red eye turned to her neighbour and said, "How can Napunyi shame us like that? Making a man fetch water? As if she is not a woman!" The one with one tooth at the front of her upper gum spat a big head of saliva at the foot of the tree and mumbled into the sky, "May her womb never see the sun again!" And they turned and resumed pinching and plucking shreds of bark from the gray stems of the tree.

Okomba heard them but he did not turn. He

continued walking. And further up the hill, as he approached the turn into his compound, he met Opyema. Opyema looked like a eucalyptus tree beside his wife who hardly stood above his waist. They were as quiet as people bearing a stranger's corpse. After Okomba had got his back to them, Opyema looked at him; his one leg sagging under the tin of water. Feeling a stone in his heart, he turned and said to his wife "the day I see you talking with Napunyi will be the end of you and me. I will find someone to follow you up with your clothes."

Okomba caught the tail of Opyema's word and inside him he agreed that if he were some other man, he would not do what Okomba himself does, "I swear I wouldn't. Unless I am not Okomba himself!"

And yet despite his incessant toiling, Okomba never raised a finger too high to risk his wife deserting him. For although he suffered with her, her coming into his life had been a dramatic rite of passage; an initiation from *Omusumba,* the village's senior bachelor, to *owedaala,* a man with a home; a wife. Napunyi had given him a name. He could now talk.

It began like this. Just one day in a dry season Okomba, who lived alone by the roadside in an old slanting house had gone missing. When people pushed open his door and found only a mat and a dented sooty pan, they had loudly wondered, some swearing he could have strayed far and overwhelmed his foot. Then the following day Okomba had appeared at the village market with a smile that joined both his ears. Okomba continued to smile even after they had left him alone. Worried clansmen, suspecting a hand of an evil spirit, had brought a sacrificial black cock and Okomba had instead picked the bird by its feet and led them to celebrate the coming of a wife. And so the people had come to meet, know and live with Napunyi.

And yet where Napunyi came from had remained as mysterious to the people of Masyaka as where the sun laid her bed. It was only Meja, the blind poet, who was an exception, singing of Napunyi's journey to Masyaka from beyond the hills of Syabwiru in Ebanda, her trudging past Nebolola, the hill of the Abahehe before settling in Masyaka. He sang of how Napunyi, a widowed spirit from Sigulu Islands escaped the vengeance of fellow spirits by coiling in a snail's house, being washed off and on shore, before her incarnation. That, wet and slimy from her shell, she then had seduced and drained youth, leaving in her trail more misery than a cow could boast hairs. And in the refrain of this song Meja named her latest victim as the father of her child Abangi. He yodelled of how Napunyi had shifted her pregnancy into her husband while he was asleep and that for twenty full moons the man had whined in labour. And that when the hour of separation came, the moment she was supposed to take back her pregnancy, Napunyi had gone hunting for cigarettes and so the baby had continued down the man, into the bladder, and finding not much room beyond it had done a *kung fu* kick. The man had made a short sound and then burst all over like a chameleon. For among the Abamasyaka, myth had it that mother-chameleon neither lays nor suckles its young; that when her time comes, the laden mother just breaks into song before bursting its young into the world.

And so Meja sang of how one of Napunyi's twins, Maya, had burst into the world and flown off while the other, Abangi, had stayed for among the *Abamasyaka* twins never die. They just fly away. And because Meja was blind and a poet, the *Abamasyaka* believed that in his blindness he saw beyond. Around this mystery people found many explanations about Napunyi, Okomba and why they had not got a child between them.

But despite all these, Okomba never lost his sleep. Every man had his own wife and Napunyi was his; every elephant must bear its tusks he often said and that Napunyi was his cross. But at times the weight was much; the weight of this cross.

So when Okomba rounded the entrance to his compound, his pace slowed down by the wait of edebe on his head, he found his wife couched by the foot of the granary with the face of a mourner. He just laughed at her. Now there was no doubt about what became of her cigarette hunting. For along the road from the well and without prompting, he had heard two children laugh at Abangi, talking of how his mother had been denied cigarettes and how her flour had been confiscated because of a pending debt. He had seen the children flee as Abangi pursued them with his catapult. It had not occurred to him that what they were talking about was as recent as today.

So Okomba was happy that she had missed but sad about losing all the flour. Napunyi did not mention her woes as she helped him get the *edebe* off his head. And he did not say a word about it as he passed over firewood for their meal. But as she fanned the fire, he saw water in her eyes. She looked the other way, and lifted the edge of her *lesu* over her face. And as she turned, he saw a wet stain down her cheek. He wondered where the tears were coming from. Was it the smoke from the fire or the fire of disappointment? Suddenly he felt sorry for her. Whoever it was, didn't they know that she actually needed to smoke? They should have at least given her one stick. I could have paid; after all she is my wife. He sighed. He then passed her another faggot and offered to fan the fire. She smiled and signalled him that it was all right; she could manage it. She bent again and blew, breathing life in the fire. Okomba always liked the feeling when they got close, and when their skins touched during day. It showed him that they were alive in night and in day; in life. And often they shared such moments except when they disagreed over a cigarette or gossip.

In spite of such lows, Okomba considered himself luckier than some of his clansmen. While at the well, he had heard that Siboli's wife, Maria, had deserted him. Okomba dared not ask the women at the well. He did not want to be called a rumourmonger. He had stood around fidgeting with the *engata* that he was preparing to cushion the water tin on his head hopping they say more but they did not. So now he wondered if Napunyi had heard about it and why she left Siboli. He really wanted to know. So Okomba stretched his artificial foot and asked, "Did you hear what happened to one of your brothers in-law?"

"Which one?" She straightened herself, sharply raising her head like a dog that has heard its name.

"Somebody's wife has left somebody."

"Now that is becoming interesting. Mh, tell me!" she straightened herself. "Mh!"

Just as he was about to mention the name, Okomba realized that he had made a fatal mistake. How could he have begun such talk about a notorious man like Siboli? Didn't he know how cantankerous Siboli could be? Didn't he know how his wife Napunyi and Siboli never saw eye to eye, except on such unavoidable occasions as funerals? And besides, this wife of his had this passion for planting rumours. And what if Siboli learnt of it? Wow! Okomba thought twice about it and instead bent fanning the fire.

"Is it Ochieno, Madyangi, Landari, Makokha? Tell me, Mm!"

"Why don't you concentrate on the supper you have not yet prepared?" he snapped, making his way outside. But she could not let him behave as if he was the briefcase of happenings. So, soon she had left. Could it be Madyangi, the thick-necked one who is always advising my husband to take on another wife or is it that Landari? Landari's wife had accused Napunyi of attempting to seduce her husband with stale liquor, and had poked her cheek with a finger saying "where would I be taking a grandfather who wets his bed?" And so Napunyi could not sleep without establishing who was involved. Possibly she had a feast out there.

So she raced. And down towards the well Napunyi

met a trio whispering and she asked them if they were talking about what she had just heard. And they looked at one another, picked their pots, waved bye to each other and hurried ahead of her. Still she followed them, planting her foot where they lifted theirs off the ground; down to the well she was behind them past the well she was at their heels, their containers empty. Two other women passed going the opposite way, in conversation. And one of them continued, "And moreover she might deliver on the way to her father's home."

Napunyi stopped.

"Even if I was the one, I would not stand a man who pounds me like a coconut." It was the one behind talking.

Napunyi turned.

The other women unaware continued, "That gizzard-headed man needs to be taught a lesson. It is good she has at last left him," the one behind the other concluded. Her stammering made it difficult for Napunyi to follow the conversation well and so she made three quick nimble steps to get closer to them.

"And you know, that man has always been marrying on credit since he was fifteen and he boasts of it. This time we'll see if he will curdle a banana stem," the other said and they burst out and laughed in a chorus, "*Hehe…Uuuuuu…!*" and when they turned and saw Napunyi listening with her mouth open, without proceeding to draw water, they each went their way quietly like fishermen who had sighted a corpse on the waters.

And so, alone, Napunyi had sat by the well. She had touched off her fingers, counting the pregnant taking off those in early months of pregnancy, those of two weeks, of one month and eight. The finger she remained with pointed to Siboli's home. The gizzard headed!!

Siboli!

Napunyi felt her blood rise with excitement. A weird sense of excitement was beginning to arrest her. If it was actually Siboli, there was no way she could sympathize with Siboli. She recalled how one market day, after she had declined to lend him another ten shillings, Siboli had publicly humiliated her snarling that in her, his cousin Okomba had married a female devil. That no wonder, women like her whose last toe never touched the ground were naturally quarrelsome. And when she challenged him to prove his allegations he answered that because her upper lip looped over the lower one she was inclined to be greedy and he concluded that her large ears were like those of a hare revealing an inclination to eavesdropping; No wonder you are such an incorrigible rumourmonger. And he said this to thunderous cheers of "You have managed her today!" Napunyi cried on and off for many days. Did he have to say all this to scare her from demanding what she was owed? She said she would die with these words, but not before paying him back.

Now at the well, Napunyi stood facing in the direction of Siboli's home and smiled. "So now Siboli's wife had finally left. If only it could be true. If only, Siboli!"

*

151

Apart from his inclination to embarrassing particularly those who made public his parasitic and treacherous ways, Siboli who lived on the other side of the ridge was also dreaded for creating stories; dangerous stories, and manufacturing crippling lies just to get himself out of financial problems. And he was bound to be in a debt of one kind or the other always. But he also had a swift hand. He could beat almost anything. He never *touched* his wives when they were pregnant, for twice he had done it and twice he had buried premature offspring.

His wives always went away and each time this happened, he was not able to cope on his own. Instead he would turn to some bizarre act to get money. One time, he had shaved his head, tied a banana fibre around his belly like someone bereaved and danced in song; *mourning* a distant relative he said he had lost. People offered condolences in kind. Later he called himself *Ojolijoli* the wise hare. And laughed and boozed for a week. He was a happy man. Briefly.

And another time when the second wife, then flowering with child, also deserted him, he had woken up in the womb of night and played the drum, announcing twins. And to the people who stormed his home, he announced that his wife had delivered triplets from her father's home. And that all his clansmen needed to do to bring home their cute little relatives, was to help him raise three goats for a ritual for their release; one for each child as custom demanded. Twins, let alone triplets, being rare among the Abamasyaka, the relatives sang praise to the giver, *Were Rachari Hagaba* the god all and fertility, for manifesting his magnanimity in a multiple way.

The folks had brought goat, chicken and grain for the ritual. Then Siboli's wife had entered, just slightly more pregnant than when she left. And three months later, she gave birth to a baby the size of a rat and people pouted their lips and said, "Siboli is a man with dry eyes." And when that baby was buried a week later, the folks said lying Siboli had killed his own child before it was born. That was before he married again and got three children with this wife that had just walked away from him.

*

Napunyi recalled all these with elation as she sat by the well in calculating pose, figuring how to confirm this before taking her course. And so when Siboli's daughters appeared at the well, as if it was the bird of fortune that had dropped them. And so she asked about their mother and after receiving the answer, she offered to help carry their water to their home; of course to see the truth with her *own eyes*, which she did.

To the first woman she met on her way back Napunyi said, "At last his wife has gone away just because a whole him cannot pay dowry. This time, if he wants that woman, poor man, he is going to vomit the dowry from behind."

To another she was more creative, "Can you believe what that Siboli man did when his sister in-law Nakhabi ran into his house fleeing her husband's beatings? ... You see, fellow woman, Nakhabi was being beaten for serving her husband the head of a fish. And do you know what

Siboli did? The fox simply locked the door and continued from where the poor woman's husband had ended." And Napunyi laughed louder than her indifferent audience. But she continued, "Siboli later said he just meant to discourage the likes of his Nakhabi from always scampering into neighbourhoods instead of listening to their husbands." So Napunyi continued from one to another, from one to another until twilight returned her home. She felt happy at what she had achieved.

*

That evening Siboli heard his story wherever he went and wondered if there was a home Napunyi did not reach taking pleasure in his woes. Reaching home, his children also told of how Napunyi had come up to his home, how she had even entered the house to draw drinking water from the pot; how she had then peeped into the kitchen to the toilet and finally the bedroom and called their mother's name thrice, louder each time. How daring! This Napunyi! Siboli wondered. "Does this Napunyi actually know the real Siboli? We shall see," he mumbled to himself and went back to the children in the house.

*

While planting the word of Siboli's tribulations around the village, Napunyi had got wind of Opyema their neigbour having brought in cigarettes for sale. She was tired and thirsty and feeling squeezed out like an orange. So with legs stretched in her kitchen, she contemplated how to go to Opyema's the man whose dislike for her was as clear as the morning sky. This man who often loudly cautioned his wife to keep clear of Napunyi for what he called "a running mouth that ruins wives of men." Napunyi knew this quite well, and Okomba had even just cautioned her about setting foot in Opyema's home. That was before he left to untether their goat from the pastures.

Napunyi unwrapped her five shilling coin from her *lesu* and stood in the doorway, thinking. Then something occurred to her; a perennial dispute that existed between Siboli and Opyema over land. That could be of interest to Opyema, she thought, her eyes lighting up.

For one time, hungry for money, Siboli had sneaked to Opyema's land and curved a grave. It was said he had buried a dog before improvising an old cross on it claiming to be the grave of his ancestor who bequeathed the land to him. Superstitious as he was, Opyema 'compensated' Siboli thereby settling matters amicably, as neighbours should. It was said that whenever Siboli was hard up he would just go and weed the 'grave,' Opyema would pay some money and Siboli would say, "Everything is ok."

Fired by this Napunyi thought: how about going and saying something about how Siboli was planning to weed the 'grave'. Yes, who would not believe that? I would win a friend, a cigarette and get at my sweet revenge! She could not wait.

"Can I have some water, fellow woman?" she said as she literally spread a mat for herself at Opyema's home.

Using her left hand, Midi, Opyema's wife, hesitated first but remembering that it was taboo to deny someone water she went in and came out with a metallic cup and gave it to Napunyi. Napunyi hesitated at first but then remembered that she was not being rude but that she was actually left-handed. And so she took and gulped the water like scorched earth. The last time they talked, Midi was asking Napunyi if she was aware of any herbs that could help her switch from being left-handed to being right-handed. She was then in tears. Her husband had given her a week to change from the female hand. He said it brought bad luck, affected crop yield, and made tensions with neigbour over any land she used left-handedly. Napunyi had assured her she could find the right medicine as long as Midi told her all the problems she was experiencing in her marriage. It was when she was explaining how her husband would not let her hold him with the left hand fearing it make him impotent that Opyema slithered in, demanded every detail of their 'conspiracy against him', and banned his wife from never ever talking with Napunyi. That was about four market days ago.

Midi was as uneasy as someone hiding a hot potato in his shorts. "Is there a problem?"

"Can't a neighbour call on a fellow woman?" Napunyi retorted and stretched her hand for another cup of water. Then, having seen a figure move inside the house, which person she took for the herdsman, Napunyi asked if it was true that Siboli's wife had run away.

"Is this Siboli's home?" a male voice barked from inside. Edging on one buttock like one easing a thorny wind, Napunyi, who thought of herdsmen as sneaky thieves who milked their masters' cows in the pastures asked, "Was

156

I talking to you? You dirty little things always smelling of the adders you steal from?"

Midi froze.

The man inside did not answer. But then Napunyi heard something like the sound of metal; some kind of pole resisting entanglement. Napunyi couldn't wait. She leapt like a Cheetah.

"You should go and eat a goat you bitch!" A club peeped, pointing at her from the hem of the roof, through the doorway. "Today you would have got what I have been keeping for you!" Opyema howled.

Then, before resuming her flight, Napunyi saw the club whirl to the left; Midi's direction "And you! What did I tell you today? Do you listen with your buttocks?" And next: Napunyi heard a brief scuffle, an alarm, a squeal, and then a body in a cloud of dust. A hand dug into a wriggling body and hauled it away into the house. Then there followed sustained wailing from Midi punctuated by her children alarming and clanging empty tins calling neighbours to rescue their mother. Napunyi wondered how she could have been as daft as to imagine that it was the herdsman in the house. Possibly that thought undermined her telling by the ear. She should have at least read from the voice. Another night without a cigarette!

And as she sat catching some breath at her home, Napunyi saw Opyema being led away by the local defense personnel; his hands secured by ropes. Closer, behind the law enforcement officers, were the local councillor responsible for women's affairs and the chairperson. Soon,

157

Opyema's daughter followed with a mat and when Napunyi asked what it was, she said her father would need it for the night in prison. Napunyi counted herself very lucky.

*

Siboli listened to his youngest daughter repeat how Napunyi had come up to home asking for their mother and how she had called the mother's name three times and then laughed *hehe wuuu!* Before going away with a smile. Siboli could not recall anyone as daring. He slouched out and stood in the darkness, faced Okomba's home and thought many things. He thumped his chest, sighed and returned inside. He gave water to his children when they asked for supper, spread for them a papyrus mat, told them to close their eyes and he covered them with a goatskin. Siboli went out again, now with a machete, but stopped mid way and returned to his bed. He slept with open eyes. He continued thinking until morning.

*

As Okomba and his family worked in the garden, Abangi grumbled to his mother about not being sent to school. Napunyi pointed at a bird on the tree.

"Did she go to school? But doesn't she eat and isn't she warm?" She then resumed her digging.

Okomba was very hungry too. He tried to lift his hoe. His strength failed and he tripped forward and sprawled. Napunyi looked at him from the side of her eye. Then after some time, she moved. She bent to help him up, but he pointed his wooden limb in her face and squalled, "Where have you been all along? If you dare touch me, I will make

myself a widower. Unless I am not Okomba himself!"
Napunyi then asked Abangi to help Okomba up.

But the boy breathed in, propped up his rib cage
exposing a deep hollow in his tummy and turning to
Okomba, Abangi said, "Do you see any supper in this
stomach? I have no strength to haul you up plus your
timber leg."

Napunyi scooped a cake of earth, aimed and broke it
on her son's chest. The boy yelled like a child whose foot
had got entwined between branches of a tree.

"Napunyi, you are a witch and you will die like a
goat, I tell you," the boy confronted his mother. "You have
refused to take me to school and you have also starved me
and your *kahusband* and now you have broken a mountain
on my chest. All because of cigarettes, but I tell you,
cigarettes will kill you before you die!" he said pointing
his young finger into her crumpled face.

"Wait until I lay my hands on you, you ungrateful
lizard!" Napunyi cursed and rummaged through the cakes
of soil for a real stone.

"Am I the lizard now?" Abangi wondered menacingly,
"Okay, wait. Wait. Make the mistake of falling asleep
tonight and you will see what your lame lizard will do to
your neck."

"Abangi, do you have another mother?" she rose,
staring at him.

"Do you also call yourself a mother? You
rumourmonger! You female witch with a lame husband!
I am going away from your home today; forever!" he

screamed with a hollowness of morning hunger.

And she threw another lump of earth at him. The boy dived for cover as the dust of disintegrating earth lifted above his head. Then he sprang up, picked his catapult and aimed. She scampered for safety and the stone hit Okomba's temple. The boy disappeared into a thicket to the left.

"Do not touch me! Unless I am not Okomba himself." Okomba protested pointing his appended limb in her face when she tried to help him up. "You are just like that little rat of yours. It is as if your mothers buried their babies and suckled placentas!"

"Who cares? You can lie and remain there until the rains return," she said.

"And how can you care? As long as you starve us and gossip about people; as long as you get your cigarettes, why should Napunyi care?"

"Why should you complain? Do I come milking you for cigarettes" she blurted.

"Try to drain my udder and see how many pots you will fill. Why don't you come and milk your bull? Eh! Unless I am not Okomba himself," and he clicked.

"Always sulking like you are half-man," she spat.

"How does that help you?" and he also spat, harder.

"What?"

"What else can I be referring to but rumour-mongering. I wish Siboli would get you for me. I would be glad for you! Unless I am not Okomba himself."

*

While the Okombas were tussling it out, on the opposite ridge, Siboli was standing with his children by the road. Having answered them that they should ask for breakfast where they were going, when an old man, Nyalola, ambled past with a stack of ropes to sell at Mairo Munane market, Siboli got the younger daughter's hand and put it in that of her elder sister and, pointing in the direction of Nyalola, told them. "Follow him till where he would perch to sell his ropes."

"And what do we do?" the bigger girl asked.

He paused, looking at her with a squinted eye and said, "Next to him, selling pieces of old fish, will be a man who calls himself Ojwangi."

"Which Ojwangi?" the girl asked again and Siboli clicked, folded his fingers and a knuckle missed the girl's forehead.

"You mean Ojwangi, our grandfather?" the smaller girl asked.

"Thank God, at least you did not inherit your mother's stupidity like your sister here!" he patted the smaller girl on the forehead. "Tell that father of your mother that since he has decided to keep his daughter; his daughter can as well keep her daughters with his daughter." The younger girl looked at him and then at her sister.

"Until when?" the elder daughter asked again but quickly stepped back, seeing him raise and angle his knuckles.

"Until chicken have grown horns and you have stopped spreading worms of female questions like your mother." And he put them on the road.

Siboli did not like his elder daughter as he did the younger one who resembled him like a monkey would another. The older daughter, resembled the mother, and he had this feeling that she may as well be Opyema's child.

Returning home and to his son Sungura, he gave him a small jerrycan and told him to go to the well. "Look very carefully and tell me all the people you see on your way and what they are doing." He spat on a piece of broken pot and looked at the boy. The boy understood, that should he find when the saliva has dried up, he would never grow any taller than the stem of the stout *Nasitembe* banana tree.

Sungura returned and reported what he saw: Napunyi and Okomba. Siboli again reminded him that being a boy he was not a woman to either cry for or trail his mother. So he sent him away to play.

"When do I return?" the son wiped his eyes.

"With the chicken," and saying this, and as Sungura took off like the hare his name suggested, Siboli pushed back the door of the house and hurried, following the path his son had initially taken; towards the well.

"*Omumasyaka* Siboli, and how was the night that kept you!" Okomba greeted when Siboli appeared.

Napunyi turned her face down to her hoe as if she had not noticed Siboli. But the way her hoe touched the ground, lightly and in fixed spot, one could tell that she was attentive. Siboli continued without answering Okomba's greeting.

"A greeting is not an insult, brother," Okomba sounded offended.

Siboli stopped. He then answered, "Your brother slept with open eyes," his brow knotted thoughtfully.

"And seeing that you have answered, may Okomba himself share a neighbour's burden for in sharing we lessen," Okomba returned.

Siboli paused and then sighed before beginning "Siboli's wife went away to her people."

"That is terrible, my brother in-law. This is the problem with these grass-hopping girls of today," Napunyi said ignoring Okomba's tapping, "or is it because of the dowry that my brother in-law was about to pay?" she added with surface concern.

"Good wife of a neighbour and a brother, she can go. Let Namukhokosi go. You see, you do not get your dowry paid by twisting the hand that is to look for it," he said relaxing and moving a step towards them.

"Ah, and should women of this village learn of her going, what a song they will sing!" Napunyi returned.

"And when have they stopped singing?" Siboli answered; thinking.

"Women will always talk," she paused. "And what are they saying, by the way?" she said with concern.

He did not answer. He was thinking about her; Napunyi.

"Then my relative should not worry. Things will be sorted out after the harvest when some money for dowry can more easily be raised. Do not kill yourself with worrying," Okomba cut in.

"The children, my brother; she went after making

sure that she had eaten all that could be eaten. And what she could not eat, she carried to her mother. Will I keep the children on my saliva?"

"What a woman and a mother!" she exclaimed like one struck by news of death.

"But I am happy that she had not learnt of a carton of cigarettes that I brought and kept in the house. What a double tragedy it could have been!" he said rather loudly as if for the whole village to hear.

At the mention of the cigarettes, Napunyi's head popped up like that of a snake whose tail had been stepped on, "Which cigarettes?"

"Fellow sufferer. Go and keep an eye on your cigarettes for once you start talking of cigarettes, the sun of Napunyi's digging sets here," Okomba said.

"I, Siboli, would rather die single on account of those cigarettes!"

"You think I will go to beg?" Napunyi said and then put down her hoe undid the knot on her *lesu* and dared her husband, "And what is this?" she said pulling out a five shilling coin. Okomba's hand flashed like lightening snatching it from her. And she fell upon him like a cat and they wrung around each other, they mingled like two unhappy puppies. And when he felt her arm getting the better of him, he cast the coin in his mouth.

"Okomba, what have you done?" and she clutched at his mouth, squeezing his jaws like a child who has jammed to drink *omlulusia* herbs. Okomba clenched his teeth his face resembling that of a grinning dog. He then wriggled,

164

making a dramatic somersault before she regained her place on his chest. Then Okomba opened his mouth wide and she peered in it and it was as hollow as an anthill hole. She glared at his greenish tongue malevolently and the glint in her eye sent a signal to him. He swiftly cast his head to the left just in time for her claws to miss a vital clutch. She could have forked out that tongue. Determined to exact her revenge, she gripped his neck and fought to trace the lining of his throat. Okomba's eyes started to pop out like those of a prawn. And seeing this, Siboli leapt forward and plucked them apart, "Woman, you want to kill a man!"

"How does he eat my money just like that? He will die today!" She flew at him. "I swear he will not leave this garden until he has defecated my money."

"I won't. Unless I am not Okomba himself!" and he tightened his muscles.

So they rolled in the dust afresh. But Siboli had seen what Okomba's hand had done. It had wound from mouth to pocket in the midst of the somersault.

"Siboli had better go and tend his carton of cigarettes, for this could be a plan to occupy me as someone is doing mischief at my home," Siboli said.

"Anyway, the he-goat has eaten my money which I had saved for a purpose. But now, *Mulamu*, I am very thirsty. For the third day now, I have not tasted a cigarette. Please trust me, I will sell some cassava in tomorrow's market and bring you some money. Give me some cigarettes on credit. I promise I will pay you before the market closes; tomorrow."

"It is not money that Siboli needs. He needs food for his children and as a matter of fact, he is on his way to Nakhamenge's home to see if he could persuade her to help in bartering the cigarettes for some cassava and grain," he said, referring to himself as if he was somebody else.

"Is that the only reason why you must wade through that river?" she struggled to regain her breath.

"They say, when the leaves and grass dry, a goat may as well scratch the ground for some roots," he answered.

"*Mulamu*," she was now approaching. "You do not have to cross the river for that; as if you have lost all relations this side of the ridge. I can do that for you. I can help you barter."

And so he had walked ahead, and she in his step, and along the way she had told him of how unfair his wife Midi was. Thrusting her hands to the sides, she wondered why Midi did not labour at the farm and raise her own dowry like many girls of her age had learnt to do. And of the women who spun rumours about him she said, "these women need some one to teach one of them a lesson they will always remember."

Then Siboli said "I hope my children have picked enough vegetables for their lunch."

"Why didn't you ask me to help, *mulamu*?" she more or less sounded like she was blaming him.

"A chick whose mother has been snatched by a kite is never too young to fend for itself, and mine too must learn to turn the earth for their living," he finished this as they entered his home. Siboli opened the door to his house. Napunyi stood outside.

"Do I have to follow a husband inside?" she asked, giggling.

"A wife must not –"

"Why, if a wife must ask?" she joked lightly.

"Don't you sense how deep the darkness inside here is? The hand might miss a cigarette and pull out another stick all together," he said, as if lightly.

"Our husband also!" And she chuckled and their laughter joined; different layers of laughter. As brother-in-law or *mulamu* the title *husband* would be the traditional endearment in moments of chiding and even more.

"Our wife, it is rather dark inside here," he continued, his voice coming from a deeper end of the house.

"Should a wife come in to help a husband open the windows," she asked.

"She should not worry, for her husband is just doing that," and a stream of light patched part of the inside.

"Yes, and a wife can now see some light peeping into her husband's house," she continued to clatter.

"The trouble is that your husband built the ventilators so high."

"Why did he do that? My husband also!" She exclaimed and giggled like a little girl.

"You know there are cats that would come in and eat his rabbits," he said, his voice sounding distant like he was speaking from a pot.

"You mean he still keeps rabbits?"

"He used to until your co-wife came and asked him to chose between her and the rabbits," he said, his voice now sounding as if he was on the inside of a roof.

"Didn't she know that you could sell two of those rabbits and pay her dowry?"

"Some people can be so foolish, never able to see beyond. Anyway, when she gave me the option of choosing between her and the rabbits, we ended with a rabbit appearing at each of our meals."

They both laughed.

"And that was not a bad honeymoon since it brought us a son, Sungura," he crossed the house to the bedside.

"Is that why you call your son Sungura?"

"Yes, after my rabbits which his mother ate." He now sounded like he was facing the wall.

"*Nga*, you are taking so long to get them. It is as if you are untying the cigarettes from the waist of a mother in-law." She laughed and her laughter sounded awkward.

"Getting what?" His voice came half-struggling.

"Eh, *Mulamu*, do not tell me you brought me here for your rabbits," she chuckled, her head peeping by the door.

"Your husband is almost through."

"But a wife's feet are aching. She has been standing for so long," she said, entering.

"Can't a wife stand?"

"And what would a husband do?" She giggled.

"I suggest you take a mat from the kitchen and sit outside." His back was facing her; his bottom distended into the doorway as he fiddled with the lower side of the bed.

"Why shouldn't a wife come in and help the husband to light the darkness inside?"

"The children or anybody could find her inside and the village will start whispering that Siboli was breast feeding Okomba's wife," he said, only his head turned to her.

"Does milk kill? And besides, who of them has not drank from outside the house at one time?"

He did not answer. He just continued to fiddle with his thing. And so she stepped outside.

"The sun is also drying up all the shade. And a husband had better hurry, if a wife has to send word of the cigarettes around."

"I think this bit will do for now," his voice came out but not him.

"Just bring the whole lot, *Mulamu*. All will be taken. I will even be the first one to give you grain for lunch. The children could even follow me right away to collect the proceeds." She moved close to the door.

"You know, I would not like to give you all the cigarettes because if you brought the proceeds at once the children might put the grain to waste. You know children are like some of you women; when the rains come, you forget that the dry season will follow."

Then there was a small silence and he continued, "you will take this lot under here first and when it is sold out, you will come for that other one over there," he sounded like one shifting a big stone. But he did not come out and she could no longer wait.

"Which lot, Mulamu? Just give me all. When will you begin to trust your wife?"

"You know," his hands were now under the lower side of the bed, "I do not want anybody or even the children to know that I have this thing here with me." He was now talking rather loudly.

"Then do not talk as if you were at the top of an anthill," she hushed him. "But why is it also taking you so long?"

"You know, I had just put the other bit in the sack and it got stuck here."

"Let me see," she said, standing behind him.

"Do I hear someone?"

She tiptoed to the door and peeped and shook her head. And he signalled her to close the door "Okay, you also be quick about it."

"Then you also lock that door quickly," he said burying his hands further in one side of the bed.

"Is it that serious?" she said, doing the lock.

"The kind of stuff Siboli has here is going to kill one of the smokers today!" he said stretching up and sighing. Then he bent again. "Come and hold here."

"You also, you fiddle with mere cigarettes as if it was your things stuck between things. You fiddle as if you are not a man. If I was your wife, I would show you how to do things." And so he told her to get her hands under the mattress, on the opposite side of the bed. And as she bent Siboli stepped back with a long thing unfolding from beneath the mattress; it was a whip curved from a hippo skin.

Some people argued that he must have used a barbed

wire on her back. Others maintained that on her chest, he must have applied a hot rod only found with the black smiths. But, anyway, everybody who was in the local court when the chairman of the local council was sentencing him and Opyema, who had also beaten his wife the day before, to a fine of two pots of beer and a cock respectively joined the chorus, assenting that the sentences were appropriate and well deserved.

Others wished Okomba had left the side of his wife on a hospital bed to be around to witness how Abangi had nearly burst the forehead of the local council chairman with his catapult after missing Siboli's nape by inches. But anyhow Okomba had stayed his ground beside Napunyi, saying only he knew better with whom to be during such a time, "And I Intend to do so tomorrow as today, unless I am not Okomba himself!"

Charming Namukati

Tabuley's mother handed him a bucket to go and fetch water for cooking lunch and he said, "*Sha*, am I a girl to put a bucket on my head!" She returned with a jerry can, which did not demand balancing on the head, and he said his shoulder was dislocated. Natocho looked at her last-born with a slanting eye and then entered the kitchen. I knew that was the beginning of a very unpredictable ending.

You don't say such things until you are old enough to look after yourself. That statement almost cost him two lunches and a supper. My mother was not amused when she learnt that one reason I had been finding cause to ferry my food to my hut was to help Tabuley survive the lesson his mother was determined to finally teach him. The sanctions had not worked. "If you feel you are now men enough, find your own homes and servants to work for you, otherwise you refuse doing work here or in the garden and I will show you that I am of the crocodile totem," mother told us as Natocho followed her into the kitchen. And that afternoon we handed someone the first opportunity to demonstrate that lesson.

Having lost the whole day tracking newcomers in the neighbourhood and getting so close, we returned home to be served sandals. Complete with the straps. I mean if someone must serve her son his own sandals, she should at least have the courtesy to wash them, especially if you know the places your son wades through. True, and we could not deny it this time; we had spent three days without touching a hoe. But what they may not have realised was how difficult it was for a whole man of fifteen and about to be seen by two brown lasses, ferrying water to his mother's kitchen. You only do that if you are going to make mud for building your house. Otherwise, fetching water just like that was not any different from bending down on the heath and using your mouth to fan your mother's boiling beans. You would rather attempt it from a standing position than bend your knees. How can a man of fifteen and about break his youthful frame, go on his knees in the kitchen? Who had ever heard of that? What would the girls think of such a one? And who would accept you to touch her daughter?

And that was actually the issue. Two cousins of Namulembo our sister in-law had visited her. So these three days, while our mothers waited for our hands at home, we were covering un-metered distances, just winding close to Namulembo's house. I mean this kind of thing of passing through the compound, returning via the nearby garden and tethering the goat behind someone's house. Although we had not said a word to the lasses we were sure our presence had been felt. I mean you do not press your shirt, starch your pair of shorts with the finest from real African cassava, go ahead to mark two sharp lines on each side of your shorts, so sharp that if, a fly fell on it, it would be cut into two, and expect to go empty handed. You do not make such effort and go unnoticed. You do not make a design of ascending squares at the back of your shirt and think someone's daughter will not gasp. "There he is!

The one and only!" So, although our mothers may not have suspected, we were investing our time outside the garden and very well.

So when we returned home, after having got so close, and I saw a full plate on my table, I had every reason to smile. What I saw then, on uncovering, was a heap of mother's symbolic gesture in a form of two large fish. Each looked like whole tilapia until the first sandal bounced off my teeth. There is nothing as tasteless!

If anybody knew what we had gone through, we deserved a chicken *combo*, complete with a gizzard. If you have never been a boy of fifteen and about you may not know what it feels just stalking someone and listening outside her bedroom for about two days and nights. I am talking about designing that first conversation with her and losing everything including your breath when she appears and getting more exact words the moment she turns her back. What's important is not only the words anyway but that she feels the words in your eyes and in the detail of your dressing. That is the stuff that hope is made of.

Even if she may deny having dropped her hankie deliberately so that she could turn around and see if you were still gazing at her, you will still have this thing; hope. That after denying she dropped the hankie deliberately, she will take off in the direction of your hut and somehow find herself inside and stranded on your bed. Or even just that she will go out for a short call at night, lose her way and end up at your door asking you to escort her to her bed, saying she fears some wizard lurking in some darkness here or there. That is hope. And so you sleep with your door open-with hope.

But, beside all this hope, it is quite another thing when you eventually get to her sister's place, sprawl in the chairs the whole afternoon and evening, pretend you have just had chicken and will not join them to supper, then stay on and wear out all the village gossip, forget where you ended and end up being woken from the chairs because they want to turn the lock and sleep. And then you just manage a "we-shall-meet-tomorrow." The two of you then reach out on the lawn and yawn and agree to disagree on who of you missed the cue to follow one of the girls as she went out to light a candle that had mysteriously blown out.

Anyhow Tabuley and I agreed that, unlike when the girls visited the first time this time round we had made real progress: we had entered the house and conversed with their host. That was not nothing. Rome was after all built in many days. But we intended to set a new world record, building ours on the second day. Tomorrow!

"Although we are going back two as we came, we have gone away with their hearts." I said as we passed the eucalyptus forest nearing home.

"Man, we missed narrowly,' Tabuley agreed, yawning.

"You should have followed her out when she went to light that candle," I said again sounding like one who had spent a whole day fishing and lost the only fish I had got when I went to wash it in the river.

"It was dark and I did not know who of them had gone out," his voice was hollow.

"But I stepped on your toe before breathing on that candle." He may not have heard me because he was yawning again.

Anyway we agreed that even if we had not told them that we were interested or even who was interested in whom, at least we had shared a moment of darkness with them. We agreed with Tabuley that we never felt as close in the spirit. We however could not agree on who was the first to fall asleep in the chairs or if it was actually true that one of us snored. Tabuley licked the tip of his finger and swore that I slept with my mouth open and that it was because of that that a blade of grass almost reached my throat. But he had no human explanation as to why he did not tap me, if we were comrades in arms, because if the grass from the roof had not woken me up, something more embarrassing could have been heard.

If it was just that there was only one girl visiting, I could have suspected the source of that blade of grass. But in this case the girls were two.

These girls were two and cousins from the same clan, the Abakati clan. A female member of that clan was referred to as Namukati. So between us we agreed and just referred to each and both of them as Namukati. So after noticing that the argument about the blade of grass was not taking us anywhere near where we had been or actually wanted to be, we dropped it and agreed that after all two promising men had done their best and what we needed was a good meal, in fact two good meals. We would then lay out a mother of all strategies that would cause the lasses to cancel their plans to go back the following day and instead follow us, just begging us to be their husbands. And we would tell them, "Let's think about it!"

I could see the one I had my eye on threatening to wear a rope if I did not marry her on the spot. "I know you may not have the cows but I am ready to come to you on credit and if my father stands between us we can sell our clothes and elope to an island of our own, after all there are many in lake Victoria." I tried to read Tabuley's face but the cloud across the moon had made the night hazier. I could not figure out what he was thinking. But from the way he hurried ahead of me, missing two-banana stems, it was obvious both of us were prancing on the springs of hope. We then agreed that the first meal was to be in my hut. After doing away with my supper we would then invade his hut and see off his supper as well; after all, that we had missed two lunches in between us, we deserved what we desired.

And anyone who has spent the whole day being fired by hope, youth and adrenalin knows what I mean. But soon we were to feel worse when we found those shoes between the plates. I was so disturbed that someone could have set aside all that time to ensure every part of the sandal had fitted under the plates. What made me feel so small inside me was that we had washed our hands and even said a prayer. Anyway later on, on closer observation, we found that the plates resembled those from the kitchen of

Tabuley's mother. We did not know of any like set on the village. It now became obvious that our mothers had been talking. This was a work of combined hands.

The following morning, as I weeded millet with mother, she did not make any mention of the shoes she had served her son. But from what she said the moment she saw Namulembo's cousins slop to the well, I knew her priorities were different. She just talked in parables about a certain breed of girls whose gene should not mix with that of her grand children and I knew that she was concerned about the height at which Namukati stood. But who told her I needed a lass I would have to mount a stool to embrace.

In any case grandfather, while talking of his ancient girlfriend, whose name he could not recall, used to say that short people can also be tall in other ways and that they were firmer on the ground. And that if they fell they did not hurt as much because they had a shorter distance to the ground unlike that other gene mother seemed to prefer. So I did not care about what she said although I could not tell her. I just continued to think my own things and when I soon complained of thirst and insisted that the water in the pot at home was cooler than the one she had brought in a jar, she knew giving me permission was like throwing a frog back in the pond. But from the way I was avoiding her eyes she new a 'no' was futile. So she told me I do not have to leave my shirt behind as evidence that I would return. "You can go wearing your evidence. I am not ready to carry your hoe and shirt back home again. But remember, the table drum does not sound twice. You are not in at meals time you get no meals."

As fate would have it those words were not much different from what she said a year ago, when the same girls had visited, and because I then thought a man should first eat and be strong, many things followed and we missed the dames. I had learnt my lesson and I intended to keep it, because when it happened Namulembo had laughed at Tabuley dismissing us as boys who were not yet men enough to look into the eyes of anybody's daughter.

Later Tabuley had revealed the girls had left while I waited for mother's lunch.

"They may not even come back," he had said, not wanting to look at me. Then his neck twitched, I think he was about to cry.

"Did Namulembo actually say that of us?" I was more worried than keen on his response.

"That one, she has eaten everything from everybody over those girls," he said.

"And she insists we are not yet men?" I had then asked still haunted by my mistake. Missing lasses because of a meal of potatoes and sour berries and moreover boiled without any salt in them!

"She meant you?" he accusingly looked at me. But I knew he was just trying to act tough.

"And you!" I reminded him. "But can't she hear our voices?" I was almost protesting trying to make my voice sound so grown up that it hurt.

"You know she is the very person who said the other

things when they found us bathing at the well. That we were... we did not have ... Anyway, you know what she said" he said with something like tears in his eyes.

"So that is why those ugly women were laughing." I had not known I was capable of feeling this angry. "Even if they are our cousin's wives, how dare they laugh at men?"

"That is the problem. She says we were not men enough that is why we were bathing in our pants. Don't you remember that other one adding that after all we had nothing to hide?" I had reminisced more than asked.

"What did they want to see? And you know what, I guess that Namulembo could have told those lasses the same things that evening," Tabuley had said, wiping his nose with leaves.

"Told them what?"

"We hide in our pants when bathing," he had answered, like he was fed up with being reminded.

"That woman also, one of these days I will show her FIRE," I had promised more than believed.

"Hoo, that one! She is mad, never try," he had sounded frightened instead.

"Try what?"

"Last week she and Magendo's second wife fell on Tomasi and peeled off his pair of shorts and moreover Tomasi did not have anything like a pant inside," he had said.

"What were they looking for?"

"Not even Tomasi knows but from that day he bought

his first pair of pants," Tabuley had said, licking the tip of his finger and swearing.

"May be he was unconscious when they did it." I had said then doubted my very words remembering crazy things Namulembo had done. So I had turned to Tabuley and said "You know what, these people can undress us. And, Tabuley, what if they... they don't find much, the whole village would know."

Tabuley paused then bent over and whispered something to me.

"Are you sure?" I remember jumping up as I said these words.

"It works," he had licked the tip of his finger and sworn.

We had to charm those girls before anybody corrupted or even married them. I had also heard from boys at school that what he had proposed worked and so there was no reason for us not to try it our ourselves. The main ingredient of that love portion lived in the *olubumbu* part of banana tree – that is the mid-leaf that has not opened up.

We were not very lucky, because mother had returned from the garden and finding you fingering her only banana tree was not the best way to show remorse for leaving the garden earlier. And the last thing a mother should know is that her youthful son is attempting to use love portions to harness his first act of love. It would break her. But we had to get it. We needed a live bat; one for each of us. So we moved on.

After considering the implications of our next strategy we went ahead with alternative B – flagging the bat that lived under granny's roof. The roof had a loop where that bat always hung. And it was not for company that granny insisted on none of us disturbing her winged relative, however tempting and low she appeared to dangle. She claimed the bat actually was the spirit of her sister that had come to wait for her. But as things stood on our side we had to find that bat. But before Tabuley could take good aim, Granny's bat was loose and out through the window. Unaware of the developments in granny's house I was acting my part of engaging her in a tactical conversation in her kitchen. I learnt of our fate after Tabuley joined us in the middle of a calabash of porridge. We switched to alternative C – her neighbour's banana tree.

Her neigbour, one of our uncles grew a cluster of *Nasitembe* bananas, these short ones that one had to bend before harvesting. So we had no problems sifting through the mid-leaves. Tabuley signalled me with his head to the where he was. From the way he was feeling the banana leaf, he had got one; a bat.

A bat's bite can be painful and Tabuley said he should be the last human being to feel the pain. But I still managed to extricate its teeth from his thumb before roasting it and taking care to get enough ashes from it before doing the same with mine- that one we captured with less pain.

With the ashes in our hands, we were separated from our dreams by one thing, finding a spot where the girls had peed and then administering the ashes over the susu spot.

Praise God, then urinals were a luxury and flush toilets a tale of the cities. Here in the villages short calls then were mostly an open-air affair. For a man, what he usually required was a stump or stem of a tree to point against, an extended wall or some sufficient bush in front of him. The women's case was much clear and easier to trace as they avoided the bush for obvious reasons. Behind kitchens or houses was a more likely place except of course if they decided to do it while bathing, something our cousin Nerima told us they really relished.

So as we marched on with our ashes, we prayed against the latter. And because the majority of women had to get closer to the ground, the spots were unmistakable and that is exactly where legend had it that you had to apply the potion, and it was said if you found it still steamy and bubbly then your chances doubled. And with the right incantations, the boys at school had sworn that even a bride would stop her vows and follow you! And that is what we were looking for. Where those girls had peed. After all, grandpa had also told us more than twice that, if a man was so desperate for a girl and weary that for some reason she might slip his desirous grip, he could call upon the potions of nature to draw such a lass to himself. We were just harnessing nature. If we could find where she had peed or induce her to, however, and then sprinkle the ash from a bat, then surely we'd fly way with her heart and hunt her by night like the bat does.

At that time, plastic bags were limited to urban shops but in the village, leaves were abundant. But these very leaves in which we held our charms also became our constant worry. They reacted to body heat, and we had to keep changing them taking care not to lose a speck of ash because where we had reached, every ash counted. So with our ashes we traversed the village always a step behind Namukati. They had this thing of moving one behind the other like naked white ants. This habit helped us keep watch in turns. I don't know anywhere we did not reach that day. Anyway, eventually Tabuley swore, from his outpost that he had seen Namukati go down as they collected firewood. The time was now!

A thorn grazed the front of his pants and he just had to slow down the tree. But when we searched there was no pool. Not even the soil from the ground, where he swore he saw her go down, smelt on anything near what we had in our mind. I remained at the spot as he went back and up the thorny tree to replay the scene. He returned licked his finger and swore that that was the exact spot her saw her bend. It is then we realised that five minutes is a very long time on a lover's watch.

I had to remind Tabuley that this was also a grazing ground with cattle and goats on the move and the last thing we wanted was to mistake a cow's pee for that of Namukati. We did not want anybody's cow behaving funny. And that is where the storm met us dissolving not only our hopes but also everything on us.

Any way that was last year when the following day, after that storm, I stayed back to eat mammy's lunch and lost a vital moment. But now a year on we had grown and Namukati were back still together like bananas on a cluster. We had to cement the darkness we had shared the previous night and achieve happiness this day. That is why I had to leave that garden. And I think mother also knew I did not need that water and hence her veiled reference to stunted genes. I couldn't wait to go right at the back of my hut and Tabuley responded immediately to my whistling. He had also seen them go to the well. And as I sat on the edge of the bed and Tabuley faced me in the chair, we proceeded according intelligence gathered that Namukati were planning to go and visit their cousin in Nebolola the following day. From here they would proceed to their home. But we could not dare climb the hillock of Nebolola. No boy from our village crossed to court in Nebolola and returned without a wound. A mortal one! I personally could name for you more than three cousins and an uncle who returned with wounds of different sizes and in different states.

Living in a place where there is no weather forecast, Tabuley came up with something we think our fathers and their fathers must have also employed at our age. What we needed was hair. Enough hair and hair everywhere! "They say girls love hair. They love hair on somebody else," he swore, licking the tip of his finger. So we had to look for hair - real hair. It was trendy for boys to go to the well and not only do the washing of their clothes there but also show off their bodies. And if one had new underpants, that presented a mother of opportunity. And they seized the opportunity with both hands, the boys. The real pants were those in the shape of mini boxers shorts. The ones I once saw Turkana herdsmen donning for a pair of shorts. Red, yellow and orange ruled the day because they could be spotted from far. So bathing at the well with new yellow pants was no mean achievement. You demonstrate that you are not only able but you could 'go across', a phrase for crossing the border to Kenya, often for smuggling goods and getting good bucks.

Smuggling was not the issue but you would get Kenya shillings, and this set you a head above the less adventurous boy. So a set of new pants at the well were always the subject on the girls' lips as they went back home with buckets of water on their heads. And if you added sandals to the pants, and especially red ones, then you were complete and at risk of getting married any time.

But marriage was not on our mind this morning as we pressed ahead, and neither did we have pants for exhibition. We had each washed our only pair and almost used steel wool to make them shine. We did not even intend to bathe in our pants as most other decent boys did at the well.

We planned to go to the next step. We were going to go to that well at the right time, peel off our pants, face that side and bathe full in the face of those girls. After all we had been reliably tipped off that they would do their washing before going to Nebolola. They had to see! These girls, they had to be shown! Tabuley said we would arrange it like an accident so that it did not seem so rehearsed. The accident was not the problem. Neither was it how to realise it. The problem was that given the distance from the anthills we were to strategically perch with our basins to where the ladies usually did their washing, one needed a forest of hair to make a visual impact on the other side. We had to improvise some hair because even between us one needed a magnifying glass to count our own. Our voices had broken faster than other grounds.

What we were about to attempt had happened in our village and even at school. We had seen these things. Boys would break into chemistry labs at school for what they called nitric acid and apply the substances on their cheeks, looking for the sideburn that would send the girls begging for their hearts. Some even borrowed handmade moustaches just to extend themselves.

But for our purposes, if we could lay our hands on four handfuls of hair each, we were sure of an impact. Our next step was to get natural glue. So we agreed that Tabuley would handle the former and I the adhesive side of it. I picked my sickle and headed off to tap the *obukhoni* sap that could easily be got from fencings of people's homes. I added a little more from the cactus type *omuduwa* and secured it under my bed and waited for Tabuley who had gone hair-hunting at the barbers. Today being a Friday and a market day at Sofia, Tambiti was certainly going to have a mixture of heads to shave. I had to keep inside my hut in the meantime. It was the sap that I had brought which made me stay. Apart from being a good adhesive, it was not only medicinal but highly poisonous.

All along I was thinking each of us was doing his part

well until I saw someone racing past our home and down to Tabuley's hut. It was Obiba with Tambiti the barber, his pair of scissors in hand, in close pursuit. Obiba's head was half shaven. They soon returned and perched in our compound demanding that Tabuley hand over the hair he had pinched from Tambiti's point. Obiba swore that Tabuley's mother must have sent her son for some unchristian purpose. It was only after Natocho had denied seeing the boy for the past two days and subsequently directed them to my hut that Obiba let free her neck. But failing to find Tabuley, they went back, saying he would be caught even if it meant trapping him with groundnuts like a rodent or with a hook like an errant cock. Then they were not only going to reclaim every strand of that hair, but he would have to name the witch who had hired him.

Later people said Obiba had proceeded to a wise man, with the head as it was, to get the name of the woman involved.

Anyway, the most important thing for us, Tabuley said was that he had the hair. Wherever it was picked from was not of immediate worry to us. "We can sort out his hair, wash and return after using it," he insisted. But I thought he should have been a little wiser than pick the lot in broad daylight; even if he was picking it from where it is normally assembled for burning. Anyway that was not our priority as we used twilight to sneak back into my hut. We had the glue and also enough hair to last us until we had grown enough of our own.

It was just that with the absolute gray from Obiba's

head, this cut-and-paste thing was not just going to fit our idea. But Tabuley's idea of black shoe polish saved us further wrangles and we soon got REALLY DOWN to business. However I had to continuously remind Tabuley not to lick his fingers as he tried to ensure each strand was in its rightful place.

And soon, even in that dim light, there was no doubt what we looked like: REAL MEN.

We were convinced that come morning our superglue would be at its best. We had not even contemplated how to get it off. Tabuley's idea was to let our own grow out, and displace the attachments one by one. However it was not as simple as that, but that is a subject of a different story as this is not the time for tragicomedies. We were however in no doubt that by the time we did catch up with Namukati at the well and do our display, everything would have firmed and even might become water resistant. Not even a storm could wash it away this time, Tabuley swore.

But before the next day we had to go through the night. We were starving. Our supper had been called off till we clearly accounted for Tabuley's bizarre behaviour. So we understood, between ourselves, why we had opted for the kind of supper we were about to roast. Fresh maize from a roadside garden!

Having smuggled embers from mother's kitchen, we got to peeling the maize very carefully, making sure the *obuyunju* crowns, what we referred to as the beard of the maize cob, did not drop on the ground. It was like stealing white ants or grasshoppers: you needed a gallon of water to gurgle and rinse your mouth just in case someone gave you cane to chew. For often the feet and mandibles of the insects stuck at the back of your tongue or between your teeth, and these lodge onto the husks when you chewed the cane. But we had to get over this by peeling, while holding the cobs over the fire, so that the flames would consume *obuyunju*.

The next hurdle was how to roast stolen fresh maize without popping it. More exactly, how to stop people from hearing their maize popping. We focused on the latter. It is not that we were doing it for the first time. It was because we had done it several times and knew what it was like; defusing a time bomb. The idea was that you sing a rhythm that required clapping, or you initiate a loud conversation that had also to be funny so that if you did not time your hand-clapping with the popping of the maize then you laughed loudly enough over each pop. We had dropped the old trick of clapping hands and claiming that we are killing mosquitoes because we were in the heart of the dry season. The question was for how long and how close might you have to peep into the fire just to have your timing right? And however much breath you have in your lungs, you might not cover as many grains of a maize cob, let alone four maize cobs as we had brought in with us.

Other than adding another case, of stolen maize, to that of the missing gray hair, which could leak to Namukati and embarrass us, we agreed to roast the cobs in a quick fire and withdraw it before a single pop. "After all the monkey does not even put its maize close to anybody's flame but we often see it play around happy," Tabuley said as he washed down his last cob with a mug of water and licked his hands again.

But soon everything changed like a bad weather forecast.

I still think it could have had more to do with the stolen half-roasted-maize than wherever Obiba went to protect his missing hair, for I did not agree with Tabuley's mother that Obiba had bewitched her son as an explanation for an abrupt stomach of the kind that followed the maize feast. Explanations that you do not steal Nalyaka's crop and survive were not convincing to me either because it was only Tabuley and I that actually knew where the cobs were plucked. And as far as we were concerned Nalyaka's garden was not anywhere near the road we passed in the evening. You needed to cross a swamp to reach Nalyaka's garden and although she certainly had a better crop, who had the time for that?

Anyway, I still strongly suspect the glue because, trust his stubbornness, he just refused to wash his hands before eating his maize and of course there was the way he continued licking his fingers and mumbling to the owner of the maize about how irresistible his maize was. Well, we could only guess what happened at the well the next morning. They must have had a lot more to talk about us. It was possibly about Tabuley being whisked off on a stretcher or Tabuley's throwing up like he would not do it again.

Honestly I did not even think he would get onto that stretcher alive. He was like a dormant volcano that had activated without warning and I just had to run to mother's window. You know how sound travels at night and how a whole village can respond to a distress call. The alarm my mother made brought in Tabuley's mother, then Tabuley's mother's alarm brought in his uncle, and his uncle's alarm brought in more alarms, until it was only those across the river who stayed in their bed.

By the time Namulembo and the lasses arrived, Tabuley's neck was as soft as a freshly killed snake. As they gathered rags and improvised a stretcher, Obiba insisted that there was no way they could take Tabuley with all that stuff over his chest. We were still our mother's sons and in emergency there is no age, there is no privacy. And however old a man, he still is someone's child. So Tabuley's shorts had to go also. Necks edged loser and eyes squinted as if doubting what the light was shedding onto their eyes. Tambiti's torch then illuminated the lower quarters of Tabuley and he swore that, born a month after his first-born, Tabuley could not have grown that fast. At least not that old, surely!

There was a still silence, one face turned to another, some mouths open, others frozen and foreheads creased. And like in choreographed motif I felt every eye turn to me. But the truth was: even I, Siambi, his mate since childhood, could not find the words.

I do not know what the girls did not say. And I no longer wonder why we have never seen Namukati again.

Maya the Man

With legs apart and bending from a fold-and-keep chair, Maya peered at the mound of *obusuma* before him, as if the millet bread was some splash of premature human dung emptied from a stomach of half-boiled greens and sweet potatoes. His hand moved and hung in the air. This was not the kind of meal he expected on a market day and on such a special evening.

Tearfully, Anyango sat on the papyrus bed tending the *tadoba* candle, which was in its final stages of life. The silence was immense. Anyango could hardly breathe. She raised her head slightly and slowly, avoiding any conspicuousness that would make her husband realise that she might look him in the face. When her eyes leveled on his boat-like shoes, she saw his foot twitch and she realised he had noticed her movement. She stopped. She then looked down. She pretended to be adjusting the dry wick of the candle with one hand while with the other she resumed rocking the baby, which was crying its intestines out from a stomach ache. For a whole week her baby son Bwire had not made a stool.

When the crying became too much, and fearing that she might be scolded for failing to make her own child quiet, she reached out again for some soap to attempt to stimulate the child to make a stool. Maya watched with a bitter expression as Anyango's hand, quivering, reached the bowl-like piece of clay pot. She drew it closer. The water in it spilled because of a jerking movement from the baby. She then got onto her knees and stretched out to the metal cup that was by her husband's feet, nearly falling over. Hinging on the elbow of the hand that held the child at a sheering angle, Anyango pulled back and poured some water into the clay piece. She then went through the process of returning the cup.

"Is that where that cup was?" Maya barked, sending her jerking. She stretched and put the cup back to where it was but over stretched in the process and collapsed on her side. She then quickly pulled herself back, sat, stretched out her legs and laid the baby across her lap. Anyango tore a piece of paper from an old exercise book with brown pages and rolled the endpoint into a cone shape. Spinning the pointed end she smeared a thick lather of soap solution. She then laid her hand on the child's bottom, opened it with two fingers of her left hand and gently sank the paper in. It entered the pith of the baby's bottom. She started spinning it, pushing it further; trying to induce a stool.

Maya spat loudly, clicked and looked back to the food before him. He dipped in his forefinger, lifted the hand to his nose and sneeringly raised his upper lip like a he-goat gauging the rear of an ewe. Through the light of the dozing candle, the tears in her eyes transformed Maya into some mirage; a monster.

"What are those tears for?" he snarled, popping out his eyes, red like those of a Nile perch. "Have you served me a corpse?" A temper creaked the muscles of his arms and his chest moved. "If you do not want me to eat your food, then do not ever bring it near me again!"

Although she was just fifteen, and having stayed in marriage for only two years, Anyango's feminine sensibilities had taught her much about the instincts of an escapist husband. She knew he was at it again; seeking the slightest excuse to ram into her, an opportunity to ferment his shame into anger and escape from his responsibilities. It had happened before, and she knew he must be having a date and that he was looking for an excuse to sleep out of home. She could not hold her tears back.

Besides, Maya would spend the whole day walking with the Pastor to the laity, preaching the word of love. One day she had waited after serving him his favourite; a meal of fish and millet bread, locally called *Obusuma ne'ngeni,,* and shared with him about her concern. "Husband, I heard that you were at Petero's home with the Pastor and the Pastor preached to them about love," she said.

"Are you beginning to spy on my movements?" he asked suspiciously.

"Husband, it was the wife of Petero who talked about it and she said it in good faith. In fact, she said she was very happy for the message about family and love," she said with assurance.

"Yes, and many people have said they liked the theme the Pastor preached about last week. For instance, Simon Odwori has also invited the Pastor to go to his home and talk about the miracle of love."

"When are you going there?" she said, adding him some sauce.

"Possibly two days from now, Mama Bwire. The

Pastor has not yet informed me," he answered between full mouths. He was more relaxed, for at times Maya could also relax and laugh with his wife like he did with other people. There was a pause.

"Baba Bwire, I hope what I want to say is not going to offend you," she smiled cautiously.

"What is it?" He was beginning to slide into rude mood. On that day he had been edgy since being asked by the wife for money to buy salt and when he failed to produce even a cent, he had argued that it was taboo to buy salt at night. And so following tradition, Anyango had just walked into a neighbor's kitchen scurried around for salt, found it in a bottle and emptied some of it in her palm, in fact enough to cook four meals, knowing how long it would take to get her own, and walked off. Among her people, it was taboo to ask for salt at night. And so such behavior as she had conducted herself was culturally acceptable. However the owner of the salt, unable to stand that cultural motif any longer had hurled abusive words relating to a useless husband who hides behind the night to deprive others of their sweat. "Salt thieves!" is the actual phrase she had used. Maya heard this as his wife walked in from the direction of the neighbor's homestead and he did not like it. So he had remained edgy the whole evening, suspecting that the wife had overdone it to provoke a tirade against him. Taking on a more placating tone, and adding more soup than was usual, Anyango had pressed on more persuasively. "I wish you could also bring the Pastor to this home to —" She hesitated.

"To do what – ?" He rarely entertained people at his home, not wanting to advertise his condition.

"That word of love, we also need that love that you take to other homes, my husband, we need it here," she appealed directly.

"Are you trying to say that I do not know how to love or are you implying that I have failed in my duties as a man?"

"No –" She was worried by his tone.

"Which No!" and he swallowed a chunk of fish and licked his fingers. "I can see you are beginning to get dangerous ideas from those women who are beginning to teach you the manners of comparing. I do not want to hear that again."

"Husband, I am sorry if you –" He cut her short.

"You had better be sorry and talk about nothing else" Saying this and without washing his hands, Maya walked away like a teacher who has been dictating his notes.

Anyango had cried. Real tears. If only Maya could realise how much of that love his home needed! She agonised, feeling like she was on chains in a middle of nowhere.

Her mind moved from one thing to another. And you should see him, my husband, in the church, his chest hoisted like a colonial flag, acclaiming those who had offered the most tithes and other contributions towards the completion of the church roof; contributions to God! Why doesn't he also seduce this God to his own home? This had always puzzled her, but she had never got the answer. Possibly God had got fed up of her unending tears and decided to turn a deaf ear like *wambulu,* the monitor lizard. Whenever Maya was asked to spare some time for his family, he would brag about his achievements and display the plastic glasses he had amassed as the most active Christian in the sub-parish. Any further complaints about his ways and Maya's eyes would swell and ripen. Maya was such a dreadful sight!

And this night he was charged. Anyango stole a look at Maya in the low light and saw her husband's eyes glaring like those of a wizard. She dropped her head immediately and blankly focused on nothing. She waited for his strong hand; for something to crash against her. Anyango's eyes were glazed with thick tears. She reached for the edge of her *lesu* and wiped the tears away. Not wanting to offend the husband further because of the recent incident when she attempted to persuade him to bring love to their home, she squeezed her nose without blowing. She then picked another of the cone-shaped papers, 'salted' it with a thick film of soap, pointed it at falling angle and continued to activate the child's bottom. The child had stopped crying. Its eyes where now open in half-asleep-motion; seemingly concentrating as if it was either enjoying the sensation or anticipating some approaching release. Maya, whose hand had just delivered a ball of food to a reluctant mouth, paused, not seeming to like what he sensed was about to happen; and immediately; *pwah* then *rrrrchwaa*! Like a tender boil it all came; the child had given way.

"Ai, What have you done?" he turned, looking away

"Sorry! It is the child." She said this, and flung the child down, tearing the book, getting pieces of paper and covering the mess in nearly every place.

"What is this?" he asked pointing to the stained hem of his sleeve. She literally dived using the edge of her dress to clean him. She knew it was wiser not to answer the question.

"Am I talking to a stone?" he barked and she jolted like someone boxed in the ribs. She felt the boulder in each of those words roll on her. Anyango's body trembled like a reed. "I do not get you, my husband," she scrambled to her knees with pleading, avoiding his eyes.

"And you say you have not got me; and have you ever got me anyway?" he spat out the words springing from the table, his foot hitting its edge and sending it spiralling in the air and splashing the food over the far walls of the room. He was now prancing around like a challenged bull. The somewhat oversize reconditioned pair of trousers, which the Pastor had lent him a week before, swaying this way and that way, like a loose mast on a raging sea. His bare feet, wobbling in the family-size shoes, caused his movement to resemble that of one making haste on a sand dune. His creased lips were resolutely pursed under his nose. Nothing would stop him from leaving the house that night; his manhood would not be challenged. Maya was set. Set to go and meet his mistress tonight. His plans would not be changed.

She saw the silhouette of a swift figure disappear into the darkness outside. Then followed a harsh thrust of the door that shook the house and extinguished the candle with one blink. Particles from the half-done wall splattered on Anyango, as she looked up bewildered by the force with which the door had been flung to. The dust from the flying soil rained in her face and into her eyes. The particles felt like sharp sand granules on her face, and she cringed with pain. She cast the baby down and groped for the basin, moved to the pot by the sleeping mat and tilted it without much care. The water poured into the basin, the pot rolled on its open side and the water flowed through her feet towards the mat and into the baby. She quickly fell on her knees. She then lowered her face into the basin and immersing it in the water, she held her breath and opened her eyes and rolled them in the water. She lifted her head, breathed and then immersed the face, repeating the exercise of opening her eyes and rolling them in the water, and when she finally put back the basin, her eyes were clear, the soil particles had remained in the water. Then she heard faint feet against the ground before the shrill crying of her baby came. She hurried to find the mat soaked and the baby wet like a sponge. She picked it up with one hand and reached for a nail on the wall, removing Maya's pair of trousers, which she then spread on the papyrus mat. Undoing her *lesu*, she reached down to lull the baby.

When does a woman rest? she thought wryly. She stuffed a teat in the baby's mouth and fought with the ball in her throat; she gritted her teeth fighting with this gauze of pain. A sting of bitter tears pierced her heart. She looked back at the events leading to her husband's outburst and walking out that night. Her husband had kept on his shoes as he lay on the bed waiting for supper. Maya, unlike always when he would hurry to remove his clothes to avoid them creasing, this time, had also kept on the pair of trousers that he had borrowed from the Pastor. And when he was going to take a bath, she remembered that he had gone along with the clothes, possibly fearing that she might suspect his movements and soak the clothes as she had twice promised. And Maya had spent a long time in the bath shelter behind the house and Anyango could hear the nylon sponge over his skin as if he was scrubbing a crocodile. He usually did this when he was going to sleep out. This now as good as confirmed to her that he was up to something. And that he was going out to sleep with a girlfriend and most likely Tina, the daughter of Mirimo.

As if searching to confirm her suspicions, Anyango tried to recall what had transpired during the day. At the village water point she had met Tina and the latter had not looked kindly at her. The way Tina moved her buttocks when she turned to go, swinging the pair this way and that way, this way and that way as if saying, "Here, here, see, see! What do you have that I do not have and in any case what can you do after all? The rhythm is in my favour." That was definitely the message she read in another woman's body. And indeed Maya had gone away from her; from her bed into another woman's bed.

Anyango sighed.

Then the baby started kicking and grunting. She realised the breast had slipped out of its mouth. She replaced it and closed her eyes. Why should another woman, a fellow woman at that, choose to take away another's man and pursue the victim with such taunting? She felt pain. "And what is it that they see in this husband of mine, that they dedicate themselves to add to my pain?" she wondered. Then on second thoughts she began to think that possibly, it is the other women who are actually causing her such pain that she begins to imagine that her husband is so bad when he could have been more tolerable. Possibly their interest in him and the things they might be telling him about me could be causing his hostility towards me. She had once heard from a confidant that Tina said Maya liked her very much. That he had promised to take her with him to Kampala. This would happen once Tom took Maya there. That Maya said Anyango did not have any salt in her and that she Tina was sweeter than ten kilos of sugar. That Tina was a keg of honey.

Anyango had got so disturbed and thinking that if the husband said so then it is possibly because they had taken long without meeting and he had now forgotten some things. She was waiting for one day when they would be together as they used to and then she would ask him who actually was better. She paused, thinking of how people can make other's lives miserable.

Because of them, he stays away from me and therefore we cannot get as much time as we should. How can I learn and even improve my ways? How can I also do some things the way other women tell me they do and share happiness with their partners? How can I grow in this marriage with an absentee husband? They are just part of the wrong company that cannot give him good counsel; and when he does not do well and provide for his child, then he hides behind anger. She recalled that, at times, when Maya got some money and could buy something for home and the child, he wore a smile. But when his pockets were dry, he became another man. I know he may not be the best husband but possibly the Tina's and the Pastor are also failing our marriage.

She swallowed a hard throat. Something cut through her heart; a pain, a relic of the anxiety she had nurtured in her solitude, anxious for the father of her child to return from wherever he had gone fishing men. She would be dying to share with him her day's experiences. These revelations of her infant maternity.

And what she was dying to say; all the words had registered and rang in her mind and her heart would sing them as if they were taped, as if they were rehearsed.

"You cannot believe it, our son heard a dove and he also said after it, 'Coo! ... coo!' " She would burn to share this day. "Baba Bwire, today the *buffalo* drank from a cup all by himself!" Anyango wanted to share with her husband every inch of their son's growth. But no sooner would she open her lips to say the first word than Maya would march out to join his fellow men, to prove to the world and his wife that he was capable of fetching his son a thorn-breasted stepmother.

O the pain that Tina has caused this home! But it is just a question of time and she will be where I am now;

dumped like used toilet leaves. By the time she realizes that she has begun stinking like some of us, we will have possibly known how to get our own oil to cleanse our bodies. She felt satisfied with that new thought.

It was getting cold. She brought forward her hand to pull the baby closer to her body for both to keep warm. She touched the back of her baby and found it exposed and cold as a dog's nose. She pulled up the *lesu* that they used as a blanket and covered the baby up to the head. She stuffed the hem of the *lesu* to the side of the boy's back, under him, to ensure it did not open. It was dark and quiet outside.

And in the still night, nocturnal winds brought the barking of dogs. She could hear the barking filter through the air in the distance.

*

The barking increased, getting closer to him. Maya drew from his pocket some of the stones he carried for emergency and aimed, throwing them in succession in a direction opposite the one in which he was progressing. The dogs went after the stones, barking ferociously as he hurried past Magero's home. "This boxer always waits when I am going to see my Tina and then it starts announcing my passing and threatening me as if someone sends it. Somebody must be bewitching me and soon she will have to suffer!" He hastened in his path. He could not wait to reach and do what he had promised Tina he would accomplish.

Maya had been dating Tina for about one year. That night when he eventually seduced her came fresh with the night breeze. Tina's mother had sent her to Maya to ask the Pastor to pray for Ochieno. Ochieno was Tina's uncle who had come under the spell of some menacing spirit. Maya and his friend Tom had offered to escort her back and along the way Tom had then talked loudly of how he was finalizing arrangements to take his cousin Maya to the city to sell in Owino, the biggest open air market in the country. That plastic paper bags and grasshoppers were now the gold of Kampala. Maya had said he would only go if Tina accepted to be with him, to keep house and all that money they would harvest in the city. And Tom said it was possible. So Maya had been dating Tina for one year now. What disturbed him was that she had eluded impregnation. "One day, you will burst with my child," he had threateningly promised.

He said this about two months back when she had started her period, tainting their bed. Maya had, consulted a friend on the art of timing and the 'expert' had told him of when a woman can conceive. Now, for twenty-seven days he had counted her cycle hour by hour and according to him, she was supposed to go into her period by midnight of this day. Watch out for the lunar pimple, the expert had emphasized. He had kept his eyes on her face and indeed he had seen one appear on her chin about a day ago. Now, it was NOW OR NEVER. If I could hammer her tonight, on this night when she is about to menstruate, before the child bleeds out; if I could when her blood is still thick and warm, I will certainly be boasting of a bouncing baby in nine months, and possibly it will be another boy. "*Yoh!*" he leapt with excitement.

He felt good and he liked the feeling. He was getting excited. His calculation was that with Tina pregnant, she would definitely be sent to his home as a wife; a second wife. "This would certainly help to discipline Anyango who wants to chain me to her side. It will show her that I am still hot and burning. *Yoh!* You get tired of one you change into the other. Two wives to Maya and that would cause sufficient competition among them, free meals and competitive care for the husband. And people will hear of it and say Maya is a needle; it pricks. And the whole village will be talking about Maya. The girls will be whispering, 'That one, he is not a joke.' "

"I must impregnate her in the next thirty minutes, yoh!" Maya exclaimed, prancing forward in a leap and landing 'Ninja style' with a rocking poise revealing the good feeling inside him. He was excited at his own thoughts and the grand possibility of the night. He was sure that this night was significant for him, Tina and his wife Anyango.

*

Anyango, still lying on their papyrus bed and breast-feeding the child again, heard the distinct bark of a dog from the direction of Magero's home. She could tell that the dog was certainly Magero's Boxer by its thunderous bark and that the object of intrusion was most likely her husband. He must be going to see Tina, Mirimo's daughter. He has left his wife and gone deep into the night to undress himself in another bed; with another woman! she sighed.

It was now eight months since giving birth to her

child Bwire. Her husband had not slept with her since she was six months pregnant, initially refusing to have sex with her, arguing that he should not have to climb a mountain. Then sometime after giving birth she tried to entice him into meeting her. Then the baby was about three months old. Maya was so shocked. He thought his wife was going mad. "Woman, you want sex with me?"

"But you are my husband and I do not see anything wrong with that." She stopped in her track, also surprised by his reaction.

"Look, Anyango, that is impossible, "he was stepping back.

"Why, my husband?" She was confused.

"Because you are still fresh from labour."

"I am OK, Baba Bwire, I feel Okay," she said reassuringly.

"Anyango, you have to come together first."

"Baba Bwire I am okay. The stitches have healed. You will not hurt me. You can be gentle, can't you?" she made a step towards him.

"Why do you behave as if you are dying for it, are you migrating?" A frown appeared on his face.

"Baba Bwire, I have healed. Even if you-," she hesitated.

"Even if I what?" he asked inquisitively.

And, smiling alluringly, she had said, "Even if you checked."

"Checked? Where?" he was visibly offended. "Where do you want me look, woman? Are you mad to even imagine that I, a man, can inspect your private parts? Do you take me for some kind of a he-goat?" he clicked.

"I am sorry, Baba Bwire, I did not mean to offend you. I was just letting you realize that you, being my husband.... that I needed you also," she moved to him, talking softly and invitingly. But he could not take it. He just elbowed her, sending her staggering and on to the mat.

"Sleep with you now and I go everywhere smelling like a placenta?" he stopped and looked back at her. "And what if people came to know that I slept with a woman whose wound had not dried?"

Anyango was not listening at this time. She was feeling a lot of pain in the side where he had elbowed her. Her eyes were wet. She blew her nose using the edge of her *lesu*. Maya noticed that he had over reacted. His elbow was hurting. He felt somewhat sorry for her but he could not bring himself to say so. He did not want to show his wife that he was soft. Would she take me seriously at all next time? A man must be hard, he thought but his tone betrayed him. It became softer.

"And you know what they will say, 'Maya is like a rabbit, just as the baby was getting out, he was sneaking in and there along a slippery path, he ran into a placenta'."

The thought of her husband colliding with the placenta inside her almost made her laugh. She fought the temptation to laugh turning away from the husband not to betray herself. But Maya had seen her shoulders move and the way they moved he could tell she was laughing or at least giggling. "Anyango, you will have to wait," he said, facing her.

"Until when?" she asked, shrugging her shoulders and turning her back to him.

"Until Bwire can stand up by himself and walk."

"Nooo!" she cried back, spinning to face him. And Maya walked away leaving her collapsing against the wall where she cried until her shoulders shook.

That was about five months ago. Bwire, constantly disturbed by fever, had not even started crawling fast. One time he had stood up, exciting her. And when she beckoned her husband to witness the good news, Bwire had immediately slumped on his bottom and down he stayed for long, crawling only once in a while. His tummy bulging with a yellow tint often seemed to be too heavy to permit possibility of locomotion.

Anyango sighed again and shifted her body slightly in her lying position. In the process, her elbow brushed against the baby and she drew her arm up to avoid hurting it. Bwire grunted, scurrying for the mother's breast with a full fist and impatient mouth. As she moved lower to give it the breast, the baby tucked its mouth into a hollow armpit. It sneezed and started crying and kicking again. She took it by its right arm, pulling up its wriggling body to the right position and pushed the breast into its mouth.

The baby pulled at the breast hungrily and then started kicking and grunting and Anyango edged on her left elbow turning to her right, to give it the other breast. For although it was dry like the other, alternating them gave her a respite as the baby would kick less. This time it greedily grabbed the breast, biting her nipple in the process. Shrapnel of pain cut through her soft spot and she felt like crying. She thought that the transfer had been within the usual time frame. The transfer was normally less costly as long as it was done 'in time'.

Bwire was now kicking. He turned and yelled, wriggling out of his mother's palm. She attempted to draw him to the breast but he wriggled away, his voice getting louder and higher.

"You, Bwire, why do you want to wear me out like this?" Saying this, she took a firm hold of him in the left palm and with her right hand; she slapped him hard on his hardly formed buttocks. Overcome by the sting of the slap, Bwire gasped, drew his breath far and then he began to cry.

He cried like one in the hold of an evil sprit.

Anyango was thrust into panic, "Mama, I have killed Maya's child!" she picked him up quickly and started placating him, "Bwire Baba, do not cry. I did not mean to hurt you, Rachala my tender one. Listen, li-steeen brave one! Do not cry like a child, you are now a grown man. Baba, fathers do not wail in their children's homes." Saying this and sensing little progress, she stuffed the breast in the baby's mouth, and then continued to placate him with other praise names:

Bwire Baba unyaKuka
The one brave son of my grandfather

Omwiwa wa'bakhulo
The great nephew of the Bakhulo clan

Owekabwodo unya'khayero
Descendant of Kabwodo,
inhabitants of Khayero

Otanyoleranga amwe mama
Do not shame me, my little father
And then the baby stopped crying but she knew
that sooner he would be crying because her breasts were
already dry. But she was tired and she needed to catch
some sleep before the husband returned to wake her up
to open the door for him. So she started to sing the baby
its favourite lullaby while patting him tenderly:
Yicha
yicha
yicha wunderere
yicha wunderere
omulesi wo'mwana
yicha wunderere
omulesi wo'mwana
badekh'enyama
mulesi kobolayo
badekh'eryani
Mulesi kobolo'lere...

After singing the song the fourth time, she noticed
that the boy was beginning to wriggle the more. She now
fished for the boy's thumb and stuffed it in his mouth. He
stabilised a little, sucked the thumb for a short moment
and then cast it out.

"My God, when does a woman rest in this world?" She turned to the child, "Bwire, where is your father in all this?" And as if the boy had been offended with the reference to his absentee father, he started kicking, turning and crying the more.

She began beseeching, above the baby's voice, "Bwire, the breasts are dry, dry, or do you want me to milk my nose for you. You know I did not take lunch. You saw how all the sauce poured when you crawled to the saucepan as I was mingling the millet bread, and the little sauce that I managed to borrow from the neighbor, I had to spare it for your father otherwise there would be no peace in this home especially after assuring him that supper was ready." She was more or less imploring the child.

Anyango had hoped to eat whatever the husband would spare on his plate but it had been soiled by the baby's eruption. "You have been here with me and you yourself added to the mess. Why can't you, at least, take pity on me?"

Anyango's breasts were now peppery from continuous pulling and wringing. Whereas she had just told her son about not eating any meal that day, but the other truth was that she had also taken only roasted cassava for supper the previous night. This was because there was no sauce for her. Maya had brought pork from the mission and did not have money to buy her some other sauce. So she did not eat the available sauce because according to her people, a woman was not supposed to eat pork. So she cooked the pork for him while she settled for a mug of water. So Anyango had not eaten a good meal in along time. With hardly a meal in two days, she knew there was no way she was going to manufacture milk just like that. But she was also aware that Bwire was incapable of taking that into consideration.

She needed sleep desperately and had to figure out some solution. And just like luck would have it, Anyango remembered a piece of sugar cane she had kept behind the pot for a rainy day. She reached out for it, bit off a piece, softened it gently between her incisors and squeezed the sweet liquid onto her teat. She did it to the other breast and gave it to the boy who settled on it hungrily. She kept shifting the child from breast to breast and renewing the surface of each teat with the drops of cane liquid. She did this until her hand could not move. When she got tired, she just stopped.

Bwire tugged the breast like a calf and finding no sweetness or milk he yelled afresh.

She slapped him harder and cast him, sending him rattling across the papyrus "What do you want me to do. To milk myself? You and your father, O' you are going to drive me out of this home!"

"Why don't you go if you want to?" Her mother in-law, Nakomolo shouted from the main house amidst the sound of a door being unfastened hastily "Do you want to kill my grandchild before you go?" She yelled. There was always something about Nakomolo and speed.

"But mother, there is not even a tear of milk in the breasts," she pleaded.

"Is that why you strangle him and call him and his

father names? Eh, what has Bwire done to you? I ask, whom are you keeping those breasts for?" She continued to prod without giving Anyango room. She was now standing outside Maya's house, her hands akimbo. Anyango could hear her breathing from outside.

"But, mother, the breasts are dry and flat," she pleaded, a ring of impatience lining her voice.

"Is that why you are stopping my grandchild to suck because you want your breasts to stick out like a goat's heart, eh? If you wanted needles on your chest, why did you marry? Why didn't you go to the city and open a shop for needles?"

"Mother why do you say all these things?" tears were close and she fought hard against a rising temper, "Mother, these breasts are now banana fibers!"

"If they are banana fibers, then roll and tie a ball out of them and let my grand- child play. Let him play with his fibers. Do you hear me? My grandchild has feet that can kick."

"Yes mother!" and she put the breast back in the baby's mouth and stuffed it while patting him and mouthing more pet names. Nakomolo continued guardedly outside, talking about how Anyango was behaving provocatively because her husband is poor and that she despises him and was trying to find an excuse to divorce. "Even poor people are also people. Who knows one day my son might get a hardworking wife, a woman of luck who will bring wealth." Anyango chose not to answer back. She knew she would have no way to stop Nakomolo.

Nakomolo could talk till daybreak. Anyango was hungry. She was also exhausted. She had no energy. She also did not want to suggest she was a bad woman and therefore to give them an excuse that their son should bring in another wife. When Nakomolo finally left, Anyango settled to squeezing the cane liquid directly into Bwire's mouth and soon he was asleep, sighing once in a while as he lay, peacefully as a lamb.

Anyango sighed. If only Maya could just give them a little of his time, then there would possibly not be as much to worry about. But what is this manhood that makes one slave for another? This manhood which walks you away from your child, your wife and your own home because you have to walk another man to places when you can't afford a mug of milk for your child? Accompanying the Pastor to gather dues for others' caring while your family starves! And you count yourself among men? Is this the manhood of our men? Anyango wondered, now beginning to feel more pity for Maya than shame.

He was really lazy. Fellow women had told Anyango that it was Nakomolo who had ruined Maya; never taught him to work because she did not want an only son to suffer. That he would grow to eat from the dowry of his many sisters. But two of the sisters had eloped and the other had died in childbirth before her dowry was paid. And his father having orphaned him by way of suicide, Maya had no inheritance to his hands. So his mother had not wanted her son to suffer. And now on account of that, he was making others suffer, she had said to herself, this evening.

Indeed, Maya, with a home to take care of and a child to raise, would wake up at noon. The day he went to the garden, when he dug, for every hoe he drove into the ground, he grunted like he had multiple contractions. Maya would hit the ground twice, walk around, come and strike it once, walk around and then he would say he wanted to drink water. He would insist on going to drink it from home and he would not return, leaving his hoe and shirt for the wife to bring. And at times, by the time she reached home, Maya would have gone visiting. And he liked visiting towards lunch hours.

He did not only visit at meal hours; Maya also liked being seen. And so lending Maya a shoe or even a shirt, no matter the size, would cause him to visit all distant relatives and acquaintances. Penniless as he often was, he would walk in the middle of the road, bicycles and vehicles giving way to him. He would reach every market, pass and stand by every stall, ask the prices of the biggest fish, the biggest cow hooves, the biggest pot of beer and the biggest everything in every nook and corner of the market and the roads leading to it. He would avoid crowded places, and choose a conspicuous point with enough space, just to show the smart man he was. And to prove that he was able and that money was within his humbling range, he would draw from his trouser pocket a beer bottle half-filled with water and soap powder, just to derive some functional froth with a little shaking, when the need arose. From another pocket, he would bring out *olugale* reed and then tenderly push it into the bottle, with a frown on his brow.

And from a distance, the market would see Maya begin to sip his drink. And then, with just enough amount of a frown on his brow, alternating shades of self-importance and casual familiarity with the drink of class, Maya was sure that he had provided the village with something to talk about till the next market day. And when he belched, Maya belched like he had been paid to do it.

And at such show times, when Maya induced a cough, which he would certainly do as an epilogue to this performance, to claim absolute audience, he would begin by sucking in nearly all the air around him, into his lungs, so that when he coughed a *male* cough, he scooped it right from the bottom of his stomach, the whole market and the surrounding hills would echo and people would say, "Maya, son of Maya, has coughed."

Anyango was as familiar with her husband's manner as she was touched to the point of always wondering why he could not confess and turn away from this sin of pretence that was killing him slowly by slowly. For without self-esteem and a heart for one's home, a man dies and so does his death become infectious to those condemned to depend on him. Anyango thought so and gasped helplessly. But whoever lends my husband these things is the one who does not wish this home well. Those who do it do not care what I feel and that I, or at least his child, need him at home like they care for their own! She contemplated this as she edged to one side and resting on her hip and elbow, she slowly pulled the breast from the mouth of the now sleeping baby. Cautiously she felt for the position of his head, reached his mouth and put together his lips. Having closed his mouth, she changed sides.

Maya would only settle after the borrowed attire had been reclaimed. And more often she had to lock herself inside the house, away from the ire of the owners of the garments who would often demand that she produce either the garments or the husband. A youth had one time made his bed first before waylaying Anyango at the well where she had gone to fetch water. He had then proceeded to drag her towards his bachelor's hut.

"Today, I must get away with something!" he said springing onto her.

"You boy, what is wrong with you?" she tried to pull herself away only for the lad to dig in.

"You think I am still a boy? You must be a visitor to this village," and he pulled her.

"What do you want from me?" she said planting quick heels in the ground.

"I know when I want something!" he uprooted and jerked her forward. At this time a ring of women had started closing in, some with their containers half-filled with water, others holding their pails at a suggestive angle.

"Mokili, why do you touch someone's wife like that?" One asked looking him in the eyes.

"Eh, and how did you want me to touch her? Like this?" And Anyango wriggled in reverse keeping her waist at bay.

"Stop being silly! What has Maya's wife done?",

another woman moved close with her pail pointing towards Mokili.

"Go and ask her husband. Why has he refused to return my things?" He tried to pull her again and two women tugged her back. A few children had now gathered. One of them giggled and then the others also giggled. When they saw some of the women turn to look at them, they scattered laughing provocatively.

"Today, I want my things!" Mokili persisted, holding her firm and twisting until her hand ached.

"Which things are you talking about that I do not know of?" Anyango was on the edge of tears. She tried to scratch his face but he ducked, freeing her wrist.

"I now do not care if you or anybody knows. What I know is that if your husband takes my things, I take his things also." And saying this he sprang at her by the waist. Had it not been for the timely action of the ring of women, descending on him with hammers of jerycans and pails of cold water, Anyango would have been confiscated in lieu of the young man's pair of socks; one small and yellow and the other loose and green.

Tired of these embarrassments, after Maya had returned and while sprawled in his sleep, Anyango had peeled off the conflicting pair of socks and cast it to the errant owner. On learning what had happened; Maya descended on her, grabbing and throwing, working her like a stubborn nut that had refused to crack, swearing to tame what he later called the female ghost of insubordination. Anyango's grip into his unbuttoned pair of trousers and his foaming mouth, as he begged for water, was what eventually saved her.

Staggering like one dangling a stone between his legs, he had almost claimed her neck with a sharp object accusing her of using her hands disrespectfully.

"How can you, a woman, dip your hand so far into your husband?" a neighbour had wailed slapping her thighs in astonishment. "If you want things to uproot, why don't you go to the garden and pull out cassava tubers. How can you play around with your life like that?" The woman had spat and walked away in disgust.

The crowd had been unanimous in its condemnation of her hand. So that evening, Anyango had been sent to her mother after the incident with instructions to learn manners from her mother before returning. She had reached her mother's home at dusk.

"Anyango, my child, how can you do such a thing; something that neither me nor any of your female relatives have ever dared; dipping wild fingers into your husband?"

"Mother, he hurt me. He nearly killed me. I had to save myself," she said, crying and feeling betrayed that not even her mother seemed to realise that it was Maya who assaulted her first, and for no fault of hers.

"You almost killed a man. What is this self-defence that makes you squeeze your real husband until he spills over? My daughter, that is not how a good woman should handle her things." the mother said earnestly.

"Should I just let him kill me? I am a human being. I have feelings. It hurt him just like it hurt me" she said.

The mother realising that the daughter was still in agony, deferred the topic till evening. She reminded Anyango of her fears, that if she did not behave as expected and Maya sent her away, she would not be welcome here.

"Remember my daughter, that you got pregnant when your breasts were just beginning to show and the people put all the blame on me for letting you get a child before I had weaned you."

"But why should they continue blaming you as if they do not know what actually happened?"

"Your father thinks what you said was a lie. At least your stepmother has convinced him so, to the point that he has stepped in this house only once since the day the village learnt of your pregnancy. He does not believe me," she added.

"That I was not raped?" Anyango burst into tears. "Mother, I was hardly twelve. With my two friends we had been invited to visit my cousin Bitu —"

"My daughter, I know the story, please do not cause me more pain," the mother said, waving her hand in the air.

" I did not know Maya then or that he even knew one of the two friends I had gone with. I did not even know how the two girls disappeared with the boys after supper. Mother, father may not believe but it is true; it is true that after Bitu had given us supper, the boys, one of them called Tom, disappeared with my two friends. I was left with Bitu, her husband and Maya. And then Bitu said she wanted to sleep. And I told her, 'I also want to sleep' and she told me that Maya would escort me to the house where a bed had been laid for me."

"It was dark outside," she continued. "I was afraid. I feared an animal would eat me. And when I told him, he laughed at me. And I said I wanted go back and sleep with Bitu and he said she had a husband." She felt a heavy stone on her heart. She wanted somebody to believe her. Her mother now let her continue without interrupting. It would help her let off the steam, the mother thought.

"And he went holding my hand. Then he started squeezing it, and when I told him that he was hurting me, he said he was holding me hard so that I do not get lost, that it was dark and an animal might take me way. Mother, it is true."

"I know, I heard it all, my child. It is true," she said watching her daughter with tears welling in her eyes.

"And then I saw him turn and face me, and I thought "O', is this man becoming the animal? He looked like *Wanani* the ogre, Mother I feared him."

"My daughter, I know that from there he tried to grab you. Why don't you just – ?"

"And so I ran, making an alarm."

"Yes, my daughter, I know that he threatened you that he would call a wild animal and tell it to eat you. Then forced himself on you. I know all what happened. Now let us stop there. You told me everything, I know." The mother moved her face in a way to dissuade her.

"That is not all, mother." She touched her mother's hand, looking down. "There is something … I did not tell you; something I have not told anybody else."

"What was that?" Her mother edged forward.

"Before that happened, as we were still standing, he asked me why I was fearing him and I told him, "I don't like you. You are bad!" And so I ran from him and climbed a tree. He went away and came back with a torch up, and he was now with that Tom friend of his. And he was telling Tom that Tom must help him to find me. And he also wanted to sleep with a woman like Tom and his other friend were doing. So they looked around and finally came to the tree I had climbed."

"You were still up the tree?"

"Yes! And then Tom said he was going back to his hut before his girl could also escape. Maya then told him 'If we do not find her, do not tell any of our other friends that such a small angel had run away from my hands.'"

"Why could he have said that?" The mother was visibly confused.

"That is what Tom asked him and he answered that the other friends would laugh at him for letting a virgin go free. I started trembling, mother. That is when a leaf, from the branch I was clutching, fell. Then they flashed their torch into my face. But then I refused to come down however much they pleaded," wiping her face, "Mother, I wished I was a boy so that I could urinate in their faces."

"My child, you went through all this and you did not tell me?" The mother complained, more than wondered.

"It hurt, mother. It hurts to think of it. Every time I think of it, it comes back as it was. It hurts mother. I try to heal from it by trying to forget, not to talk. I did not want you to feel the hurt too. They blamed us for everything. Some people told me a woman is a pot that must bear. I saw Maya as my fate." Bursting into tears, "Mother, he killed something inside me."

"Do not cry, my daughter, tell me. Tell your mother everything they did to you. Get it out of yourself, my daughter." She fought back tears. She wanted to remain stronger than her child, for the sake of her child.

"On that night when he hurt me?" she said, recollecting

"Yes on that night when he hurt you."

"So when I refused to come down the tree, Tom said they had to change their methods. He gathered grass around the tree and asked for a lighter so that they could smoke me down."

"They did that? And, how old were they?" she was disturbed.

"I do not know, mother, but they did these things and they knew what they were doing. And, mother, when I saw smoke climbing the tree I started crying, and I jumped down?"

"You fell from up a tree, Anyango?"

"And into their hands, mother." Her voice was now shaking. "And they carried me away… and I cried 'please do not do anything bad to me. Take me to Bitu; take me home to my mother!' But he could not listen. He…he…he hurt me mother."

Anyango's mother was very hurt her daughter could

have gone through and lived with this in silence. But how could she and the others have known when they were so blinded by rage? Some had even laughed at her when she said that she had run away after she had been raped. They said "there is no way one can conceive when a man sleeps with you for only one round. Even if it is a venereal disease, you cannot contract it in one round. Pregnancy and venereal diseases come only after things are repeated. She is just pretending. She knows those things." They had called her a shame to the home and asked her to go to the home of the one whom she shamelessly bared herself under. And so Anyango had been sent away to find Maya, her man. Being so young she had failed to bear the baby. She lost it and she nearly died in the process. How Anyango's mother now wished she had known the detail! She would not have allowed her daughter to become a wife to such a man. She should not have got a second pregnancy by him. But she refrained from mentioning this matter as it always caused the daughter agony. She hardly ever referred to it and the mother let it rest at that.

"I wish I had not judged my daughter harshly. That dog of a rapist would have been taught a lesson," she reproached herself, now seeing her daughter in different light.

"Mother, I did not go looking for that baby, I swear. I did not know what Maya was doing to me. How could they blame you or me for it? Mother, how, how?" She burst into tears collapsing and burying her face in the lap of her mother. The mother pulled her up, supported her and held her close to her chest as she used to do when her daughter was still a baby; not very long ago. The mother's face became wet too and she let emotion and all flow freely down her face.

When their emotions eased, they talked into the night. She told her not to let him hurt her again.

"How, when he says he paid for me?" she said, more as a statement than a question. "What dowry is he mouthing about? The fifteen thousand that fetched those limping goats; only two of them and he wants to kill you for that? The time you come back to visit me again, I will have raised fifteen thousand shillings, the equivalent of his goats. You will have to keep that money and should he disturb you again, you leave it on his bed and come back home and let us see how he will come to claim you." The mother was visibly shaking with emotion.

"I come back here? Won't father kill me?" There was fear in her voice.

"He will have to kill me first. And after all, I will have paid back the miserable goats which your father, himself, drank in a week."

But after a week at home, their tempers had cooled. Her mother's sister had learnt of Anyango's return and had come to see her. She had convinced Anyango's mother that they should give Maya another opportunity. That Maya, being a youth, was partly influenced by his peers. Anyango's mother remembered how hot-tempered her husband had been when they had married and how he had cooled down like the setting sun. So the aunt persuaded Anyango to go back and apologize for reaching out for her husband's manhood.

She knew that although her niece was abused and offended, as mothers it was their responsibility to help her make a home. She had taken her niece aside and admonished her that marriage was made and not simply declared or just found. She said they should be mindful of the community in which she lived where girls who failed in their marriages or had children outside marriage, who were looked at as spoilt and the best they could hope is settling for the status of a co-wife. And in their society women may not be allowed to walk in with children from another relationship. "The greatest virtue of womanhood is perseverance. Every home has its problems," her aunt had assuaged her. "Do not let the secrets of your home escape through the roof. Marriage is a mat that you the woman must weave."

"Even when I am suffocating mother?" she asked.

"Come back home here or to my home in Boolya for some fresh air. You may not yet know my child, but men do not grow and neither your tears nor sweet promises from a woman will change them," the aunt said.

"And why should anyone live with someone who never grows?" Anyango wondered.

"Child of my sister, these men are like the soil we work, tread and bury our dead in; they are everywhere and the same. We cannot walk without stepping on it. Or shall we pack our feet and lift them to our heads because this soil will make them dirty? My child, what we will need as women is to make sure that we make a journey to the well and keep some water by ourselves so that, at whatever time that soil makes contact with us, be it day or at night, we always have something to wash ourselves inside-out to keep our selves clean; to renew our hope.

Later that day, the last day with her mother since she had been sent away, her mother gave her a basket of flour and a cock to go and cook a reconciliation meal for her husband, as custom required. She cooked and ate with her husband Maya. And when they got to their papyrus bed that night, they were able to catch some sleep only towards morning.

After the reconciliation, things had seemed okay, but just for some time before Maya became himself again. It got worse after the death of their first child who could not pull through labour. It was a boy and he thought the baby's death was a bad beginning for him and Anyango. He started chasing one girl after another and returning towards morning. It had continued to happen even after the second child had come in. She was still lying alone, to this day, except that this night she knew for certain whom he had gone to sleep with; her archrival Tina.

A dog and a cat fought a brief battle by her door. If they pushed any harder she was certain the door would give way. The baby woke up with a start and she softly patted him to sleep. Anyango feared nocturnal sounds. She would scream and call Nakomolo for help. But this time she did not feel anything. She heard the cat purr and a dog yelp and then, their running recede in the direction of Nakomolo's hut.

"Mukombosi. I am talking to you, Mukombosi!" The

growling of the dog stopped. "Has Maria become your wife?" The dog growled again. "Have you become deaf? I know how all you male things in this clan despise us, but if you do not stop chasing my cat Maria, I will harvest that scanty tail of yours and we see what you will call yourself." Anyango lost the rest of Nakomolo's words to a harsh wind that was beginning to brew outside.

Nakomolo would always remind Anyango that, as a woman, she was supposed to help mould and make her husband. But how does one mould Maya? Or better still, how do you unmake that man? And by the way who made him? She wondered. And then something occurred to her: what was Maya anyway? What was he in her life? What did he do except sleep on top of her and abuse her? What else had he done other than impregnating her, impregnating her and telling her to always remember that he was the first man who did it to her. Reflecting on these issues Anyango began to ask many questions. She was beginning to feel strange. She touched her own arm and for the first time she seemed to sense her presence. She was there. But where was she, where had she been and how did she reach where she was now? Was this the end? Is there something like the end? Is it just because of a child? He had never claimed that much of influence until she carried his baby and then when it happened; everybody had known her as his wife. Where does my life as Anyango begin and where does it end? Is this my eternal position, under a man? Could it have been different if it was Tom or another man? What is it like being on top? Can't I climb and get on top of him?

Would he accept and what would he look like looking up at me and me down, down at him? Eh, what happens if I did? Possibly he would peel off like it happened with Gusino when his bride lay on top of him. They would possibly say a woman slept on top of a man. Yes, if he finds that dangerous we could try it side by side-same level and no cheating. Possibly then we can talk with our eyes at the same level. Yes who wants to be down? To bear the weight of another, bear the weight every night for the rest of one's life; with an imposing beast on you and all over you? Always bearing an unappreciating baggage even if you are lighter, even if you are disabled, even when you are sick, even when you do not want to move, the baggage says move and you have to move?

She now recalled his twisted face and towering mass over her little self with a helpless pregnancy in between. Does it take a normal person to lie over a mother and the baby? Lying on their own babies? Why can't he also carry you and you share and alternate a shared weight? She could not understand where the questions had appeared. The questions were becoming many. But they are possibly many because they have been gathering inside, possibly because I never got a chance to think about some things. She was now sweating. She sighed. Although it was dark, Anyango closed her eyes and continued, thinking.

Outside the wind got stronger. It blew and the roof of the house creaked. Blades of grass from the blinking roof and the loose soil from the termite paths drizzled on to the floor. Anyango hurriedly figured out where the baby was and covered its head to avoid the debris going into the child's face.

And so I have to be a woman! I have to behave like a woman so then he can feel like a man. Anyango found that she had already sat up and she was now sweating profusely. Why had she never asked herself these questions, she wondered again? Why not before? Where was her stake in this relationship? What could she call hers except the fifteen thousand shillings that her mother had given her to keep as an emergency refund in case she found the marriage impossible? Thinking of it, she got up, climbed on a chair and reached up to the roof. After feeling around, she found the cloth in which she had wrapped the money. She felt the knot and it was as she had tied it. She sighed. She felt there was something from the very heart of something but she could not just figure of what exactly.

The dog and the cat again came, growling and purring towards the house and the sound went round the house before filtering in the bush beyond. That is another Maya in this home, she thought, wondering what stories they could tell if she got to sit with the cat and talk. Is there something wrong with male things? Why doesn't that cat go away? At least it has no child or relative in this home. What binds incompatible things? She wondered.

Marriage is not an association or a carcass to be shared out. That is what her granny had admonished her when she came for the funeral of Anyango's baby. It is not a competition, Anyango my grandchild, marriage is a delicate basket in which you have to bear your water patiently through the hills of womanhood. That was her counsel. But sacrificing for whom? Where does sacrifice end and where does co-operation begin? When is marriage a marriage? She was confused. Should she believe the elder women or respond to the challenges of her growing self? Anyango felt as if her heart was going to hatch into a swarm of locusts. She sagged; hollow. She was spent. Her throat was dry. She fixed the money back into the roof, and slumped into a heap on coming down the chair.

She crawled to the pot and drank cup after cup of water until she could not find breath to continue. Having drunk, she felt a bit better and walked to the stool her husband had been sitting on. She sat and cupped her head in her palms. Inside her, a certain consciousness was beginning to crystallize. How does she begin getting answers to the questions? Whom does she ask? Who will listen? Must somebody listen anyway? She felt more helpless and fresh tears began welling up in her eyes. She attempted to get to her feet but lost balance and staggered to the wall. Anyango paused for some time and after gathering a bit of strength in her limbs, she supported herself on the wall, wobbling along until her feet touched the head-side of the mat. She lay down on her back and stared through the glistening roof.

And how do I proceed with and after this? What do these questions mean for my child? What do the answers hold for me? And what of Maya? And does he also ask himself these questions? What if we shared them? But can we? She sighed.

Then she thought, however bad Maya was, he was still her husband and the father of her son Bwire, I know that I may also not be the best as a person, but at least I try. I care for you Maya. Tom touched my breasts this week. He squeezed them. I began feeling funny things but I told him to go away. I could not bring myself to sleep with another man who was not my husband. I did not want to hurt my husband. I must confess Tom's hand was not hard. But I could not. "Bwire, I care for your father." she found herself whispering towards the baby. Yes, the other truth is that people are also just using him? I wish they paid him something for walking around with them. There are times when he comes home with a piece of sugar cane for me or with a mushroom he has picked along the roadside and I cook and we share it. I do not think he was as bad until the Pastor and Tina came in. They are the ones actually helping to kill my home, my child!

And she broke down and cried for him.

There was certainly something that was getting wrong with Bwire's father and she wished she could cure him of some of these before it caught up with the child. I care about your father. I even wonder if I should blame someone else. At times he defeats me. Some of the things he does are those one could normally expect of one who has been bewitched.

Indeed Anyango felt that Maya needed more prayers for his restless hand than for his soul. For wherever he went visiting, Maya returned with used pieces of soap. But which is this market that sells second-hand pieces of soap? And in the heart of the night? Anyango had begun to smell a rat. Could these be leftovers of what was used to wash the Priests' cassocks? But whatever the source, she was now almost certain that soap smuggled in, in the womb of night, after visiting other's homes, was born of dirty hands; hands that needed washing. And where could he have picked up this habit.

The wind shook the trees outside harshly and Anyango crouched for the baby and waited, fearing that this time it would go with the roof of the house. An iron sheet clanged, and then a rolling stone fell to the ground. She closed her eyes and waited for the worst of a wizard. Nothing happened. When she opened her eyes a big hole glared at her through the roof. Anyango could clearly identify the constellations in the sky. The wind had blown off the sheet and stone she had personally put on the roof. Maya had never thatched the house apart from the temporary mini stacks that he had thrown on the roof when the house was being constructed; two years ago when she came to live with him. It was getting colder. She quietly lifted the baby to her shoulder and pulled the mat to a less exposed side where she and the baby now lay.

Anyango's life was that of from-pain-to-worry and then to pain and to worry all her day. For no sooner would one worry subside than another wave would surge in. There are things that she felt that as a man of God, Maya should have kept his hands and heart far from. There was the Sunday morning when Maya had left to greet his cousin Tom who had come from Kampala. After this, he was supposed to hurry to church for the morning service. But no sooner had Maya gone than his wife saw him return, clutching his bible close to his breast. It looked like he was protecting something from view. After entering their house, he had immediately emerged and gone away; this time in the direction of the church.

Something caused her to check on Tom to find out if there was anything the matter. She had found him throwing his bed upside down, definitely looking for something. But she could not ask what the matter was, partly because she did not know where to begin and also because it was in the morning and Tom was in a short towel. And she had heard quite a bit about men and morning erections. And that afternoon Tom had come to her to find out what she really was looking for that morning. That is when he had held and squeezed her breasts.

"That night, my husband entered the bed with a used pair of underwear smelling of town perfume," she recalled with a clot of pain in her throat. She felt very ashamed. So much ashamed that she could not look into the mirror for a long time.

Ashamed as she felt whenever she met Mirimo, the village second-hand clothes dealer and father of the girl who became her arch-rival. He does not only know how poor and useless my home is but knows as well as everything about me right from the bangle on my wrist to the last scar on my body. She was convinced that this was true and painfully so. No wonder his daughter despises me. And it was for that reason that she never could amass courage to confront Tina. Tears filled her eyes, as she recalled how she had gone to Mirimo's home with fifty shillings, only to be told that the inner wear she had come to purchase cost thrice as much. She had given up the hope of ever wearing one. But the gossip of the women at the well and in the market places, creating riddles and twisting tongues about a young man's wife whose skirts were always tucked between the valleys of her hind hills, hurried her back to Mirimo's home. And so, Anyango had thrown in her whole heart and cried for two days until Mirimo took pity on her and accepted to let go the big blue pair of hand assembled knickers, which had been lying in stock for the past three years. In fact it had been given to Tina's mother who in turn gave it to Tina to deliver it to Maya. Then, Tina had not yet known Maya in a way to cause worry.

With its prominent string around the waist, it perfectly resembled a lose pair of shorts. Fifty shillings plus five cassava tubers was not a bad bargain, particularly as a rat had burrowed as sizeable hole in its rear.

Nature's ways led her from one conquest of fear to another. For although still young, and vulnerable, one thing she was so conscious of was public opinion. For whether a good or a bad bargain, she was haunted with the pain of shame. What ached her was not her having nothing as people knowing that she had nothing; nothing to the last corner of her body. She remembered how one time a maniac had entered the evening market and sent it helter-skelter. While others took off for their lives, Anyango fled for other reasons; the fear that if the lunatic suddenly stripped her: lo, what a sight! She said to herself 'I must get something decent, for, one day, I might fall sick and be in a helpless state. I should not shame my husband.' "You can tell a woman by her knickers," her mother had once told her.

In an attempt to set her nerves at rest, she had taken some of her millet to Lukhoni market and returned with *Tajiri* pants. The moment she had shown them to her husband, Maya's eyes had shot out. How do you buy knickers without consulting me? That was the sure reaction she helplessly awaited. But instead, Maya had simply peeled off the old pair she was wearing, put them on and, in a soft voice, he had mused. "How could you have two when a man has none? Is this the equality you women are talking about?" And he laughed and turned, hollow eyed in the rear, revealing the confluence of his papyrus-marked buttocks.

And from that evening, he had not put them off except when she felt they needed washing and this she would do in the interest of fresh air. She sighed and turned to the other side and covered her face in shame.

*

You should feel ashamed! That is what his wife had once in a while managed to tell him. Ashamed of what? A man should not feel ashamed of making his position felt. That is what he had always intoned to himself. And this night, as he turned from one bend of the road to another, he did not see why he should feel ashamed of heeding the call of manhood, he said, adjusting his wife's knickers, which had lodged in his bottom.

Ahead of him, Maya could see the big Muvule tree that always marked the beginning of the last part of his journey. It was huge and dark, its branch hanging low. A carpet of leaves always covered the ground under it. It was said to be a dangerous spot, not so much for the leopard that was killed there some years a go but for a notorious wizard who would catapult himself onto one of the lower branches and with a rope loop it around the necks of late travelers, yanking them up and releasing them in instalments. Some said he was a sadist while others said he was an unsuccessful cannibal. But what all agreed on was that he would laugh in a husky voice as he dangled his victims up and down. But this being the shortest route, Maya had to go via it. To beat the wizard, just in case, Maya bent to the level of an average village goat, lower than he gauged the rope could be looped and then waddled quickly past the tree, like a duck. When he stopped, he had so much pain in the back that he had to get to the roadside and lie down on his back for a moment. He knew this was still a dangerous place but "there is no way I can go to meet her with a broken back," he told himself. He pulled out a bitter herb from his pocket and started chewing it to keep awake. He did not want to finish it, as he needed it more for the night.

A man does not let a woman govern his life. Mm? How do they hear that I, Maya son of Maya listens to one who cannot urinate in a standing posture? The voice inside him laughed derisively as his feet accelerated with charged lightness. The mark of manhood is about being unpredictable. All these feelings and thoughts stewed now in him as he left the overgrown path to join the main road. You keep beside a woman most of your time and she struts among her kind, thumping her hairless chest 'He is now here!' pointing under her armpit. So he maintained this position of what to him constituted a perfect grasp of the female kind and its inherent inequities.

"*Yoh!*" he exclaimed, jumping a pothole.

"Grandfather never kept by their side. Never! That is why, by the time his voice broke, he had impregnated five women whose breasts were just beginning to wink through their chests. Yes, my grandfather, like a real man, had villages of land and animals which, if you needed to take count of, you would have to wake up early and have a real meal of potatoes and beans and after that proceed to climb the tallest tree to view them well enough. All these to himself!"

"*Yoyo!*" He jumped two potholes.

He mumbled and swore, "I will not be like my father, who had nothing to show to posterity."

He was now sprinting.

I will not let this bright moon shine on the chests of other's sons while I lie at home as if a dog died on me. I will be man.

He discovered himself a few inches from another obstacle. And before he could ascertain whether it was another pothole or a shadow from roadside foliage, one of his feet had slid ahead of him. The other folded too and jerked him forward and by the time he decided not to move, his limbs tangled, and he managed a trip-over landing. "An ill omen!" he mumbled as he stabilized with the right foot in the shoe and the left one bare. The left shoe had remained in the pothole and his bare foot hung, suspended in the air like that of a cock under a shade in a hot midday sun. He looked back through the near translucent nocturnal light and saw the shoe. It lay on its mouth; its bottom reflecting muted peelings of moonlight like tinted glass. It was then that he remembered that in a hurry to leave home, he had forgotten to stuff some rags in the rather oversize shoes to make them firm.

He felt like spitting in his own face. He was now losing time because of this omission. No, it is not my fault. It is this damn woman again. It is the silly woman with her nagging and this madness to limit me to her; to one woman, that bears me this curse. I have never been happy since she failed to push out my baby. He hissed, cursed and spat a baby head of phlegm on the ground. That woman!

He shook his fist in the air and pointed a finger in the direction he was coming from. It had feeling.

She must be conspiring to give me a love portion or even bewitch her potential co-wives; a cynical smile rimmed his lips as he toyed with this realization of his own. He sighed and paused. He then folded his left leg and hopped towards the side of the road for some leaves to stuff in the shoes. As he bent to pluck them, he slipped over a slimy substance and scrambled onto all fours. The freshness of the texture beneath his right hand jolted him up. His hands were damp with something warm, soft and wet.

"*Yoh!*" he turned away his head like one that had

bumped in his mother in-law. "Damn the he-goat who eased himself in the middle of the road!" he cursed, wiping his hands on a trunk of a nearby mango tree, before rinsing them in the dew that had started settling on the fleshy *amatulatula* leaves that lined the road.

Like one trying to identify a more tolerable toilet, Maya smelled his hands with a tilted neck. "*Yoh!* This he-goat of a Pastor with his grinding club of a heel!" he cursed pushing his foot in the shoe. "How can a man of God have such a well of a foot? Can't he have the sense to buy various sizes of shoes, after all he gathers from the poor and the dead?" He rolled his tongue to click but a more serious thought stuck it to the roof of his mouth. How can you blame this man of God? They give charity. They have bought blankets for the old and they are now building a school. You are at fault. Maya, if you had married a second wife, this would have sobered Anyango and taught her to work harder. This competition would generate wealth for you. His mind twitched. And with that, what shoe couldn't you afford?

"*Yoh!*" Maya exclaimed making successive baby sprints in the air. Sprints of elation. "I must talk over things with Tina tonight."

He leapt over three potholes in one motion.

A drunken voice filtered in from the distance, and Maya thought that that was most likely a coward, but more or so he realized that time was running out. He had to double his pace to be there before people stirred from their first sleep. For then he could comfortably steal his hand through the ventilation above the door and disentangle the long pole plugged under the mid-door support. He would then push his way through without disrupting the quiet of sleep. "Just a matter of time and I will be beside you!" he whispered, letting the wind carry his words to her as he followed, entering the last leg of his four-mile journey.

*

In her bed, Tina lay on her back; her stare lost in the void. Inside her mind, many things were happening. She was desperate about her boat that had capsized when the shore was just an oar away.

For the morning of today, unlike other days when her mother, Namayindi, would rise at dawn, stand by the door and repeatedly yell out at her to wake up and go to the garden, Tina had slept with one eye open. And at the first crow of the cock before Namayindi came, Tina had picked her hoe and hurriedly sloped to the Swamps of khayero to heap the famous *Sunjuchu* potatoes. By the time the sun woke up to smile over the hills of Ganjala, Tina had already finished half of the day's digging. Unaware that her daughter had learned *good manners* that day, Namayindi had called and called until her voice had almost gone; only to reach the garden and find a most hard working daughter. She almost regretted that she had not entered to check by herself. But on second thought, Namayindi realised she was wise not to have risked that. At first, she had got into this habit of calling only once and if the daughter did not respond, she would ram into the house and peel off Tina's blanket. But one day, from between the blanket and a crouched daughter, a wet man had scrambled through her legs. And from that day, Namayindi learnt to keep an appropriate distance when it came to dealing with grown up children.

By the time lizards and the expectant began withdrawing from the biting rays of the sun, and the sounds of cowbells receded into the pastures, Tina was lifting a jerrycan of water to her head. It is then that it occurred to Mirimo and his wife that their daughter had fetched water in advance and kept it in the garden with her. They exchanged looks. When they turned to look back, a jerrycan was winding its way uphill amidst the *obengele* shrubs.

Mirimo sighed.

"I will catch him!" he swore gnashing his teeth like one chewing corn and sand. He did not look at his wife.

"Who?" Namayindi asked looking aside.

"You will tell from the direction of the mourning," he said as he sharply pointed a harsh finger beyond the horizon. Although she pretended not to know, Namayindi was aware that her husband was referring to the Pastor whom he believed was the man spoiling his daughter Tina.

I wish you knew who scampered through my legs when I had gone to wake your daughter, you would not continue insisting that Maya was merely running errands like he did not have his own leg. She laughed at him from inside herself.

Mirimo and wife had returned home to a ready lunch.

There was enough water too. Namayindi knew this was not for nothing. But if Tina was not careful, that night, her father was going to fell a man. Of this she was sure.

Tina waited for Maya to prove to her that night that the sun he said shines from her was the light of his world. And now that Maya had told her Tom had found him a job in the city, she was tired of the village and she would ask him that they go to live together, leaving Anyango to till the land. Maya had told her the days of touching a hoe were numbered for her and that her work would be to eat, bathe and sleep. Servants would do the rest, he had added. "As for food, if you get bored of meat and rice I will be sending a lorry to collect food from the village every weekend," Maya assured her saying he was not able to make much progress in the village because his wife had the worst *kisrani* of bad luck. "She does not have a hand of income. Hers is the hand that takes out not one that brings in. But I know that you are different. I feel it when I am with you." And that Tom was arranging everything. Now that she had seen Tom around, she would ask Maya when they would be leaving and what she should wear on that day.

So in preparation, Tina had bathed and gone to the evening market an hour earlier than usual only to return and find Ochieno at home. Ochieno was a distant cousin to her mother's. Ochieno's impromptu visit was not for the love of his kin. He had returned to seek the cure of a wise man, Ombugu. Wherever he would turn to walk, Ochieno claimed he heard calculating footsteps behind him.

The night had caught up with him on his way to

Ombugu's shrine and so he had branched to his sister's place for a night before proceeding to Ombugu, famous for his skill in luring stubborn spirits into his magic guard where he was said to trap them, the spirits screaming of aching bones and pepper-hot arse while Ombugu would take his time suffocating and decimating them.

All those who had seen him arriving agreed that from the burrows on his face, Ochieno was a famished man. Ombugu had told him to return, after three markets, with one strand of gray hair from a childless old woman and a hornless ram too. Or he would have to bring a gray strand of hair from the crotch of a woman of his mother's clan. In addition he would accompany the elderly hair with a black bull and a milk white cock. But from his look this evening, it appeared like the footsteps were getting closer and closer and Ochieno must have decided to reach Ombugu before they caught up with him.

Because Ochieno was an in-law, Mirimo instructed Tina to leave her bed for the visitor and transfer to another house, that of her brother.

There was no way Tina could reach Maya to let him know of the changes. So behind her brother's house, Tina was squatting against the wall looking directly to her left where Maya said he usually entered from. To her right there were banana trees and under the trees she had made a quick bed from banana leaves. Tina had been waiting for an hour. She began turning. Her legs were now aching. Abdominal pains were now setting in and a migraine could be felt. She realised she had also been out in the cold for long without covering herself. She mumbled a few words cursing Ochieno for invading the warmth of a bed she had laid and prayed for as early as midday. She wished the footsteps could catch up with him, that night once and for all as she slumped on her bum, leaning against the wall and whining again.

While she was waiting at the vantage point for re-routing, Maya had been very creative. This night entering the home through a hole in the fence, he crept past the kitchen and stopped behind the usual hut. He surveyed the direction of the main house, just in case. Satisfied, he bent to avoid the low hem of the roof. He crawled along the wall. Something cracked and he stopped. Tina run into the house on hearing the sound thinking it could be her father. Her sister in-law had agreed to leave the door open. Tina pushed it back slowly before tiptoeing to her new bed in the sitting room.

When Ochieno heard something break under a foot outside, his hairs stood. His heart stopped. He felt the heat of adrenaline in his mouth. He tried to reach for his clothes. Something creaked. He was not sure if it was his bones or the bed, and he thought twice about moving. Nothing more came.

Where does a single footstep end? He wondered. This must be the thing. It is now beginning to assume a certain unpredictability. His predicament had begun with this funny feeling of somebody following him. Then he had moved to squirming in his rest and his wife had complained of his kicking in his sleep. Then he had run to a wise man that told him it was the spirit of a corpse he saw while fishing that was following him. For one day, while fishing with friends on the lake, a floating body had been sighted and one among them had called Ochieno's name, drawing his attention to the disfigured mass. And because his name was called and he did not rescue the corpse, its spirit followed him, so it was explained and he strongly believed it. Then soon, he said he had started hearing someone running after him. So he had run and run to the wise man's place and he had been given medicine. Then that the spirit had changed to following him in long strides, then to short crispy steps which were getting more nimble and closer every time he listened more carefully. And now tonight, this night, Ochieno had heard just one stride.

"When it comes next time, it will come to go away with someone." Those were the exact words of Ombugu. Ochieno's heart quickened as the diviner's last words came to him with astounding revelation. Something gave way in his interior. The walls of the house started thinning. The room became smaller and smaller. He now sensed deliberate strides closing in on cotton padded steps.

Then everything seemed to listen. It was the silence of a diviner's shrine; a sensory surveillance of a hunting spirit, a hungry spirit on clear assignment.

The door locked from inside. Ochieno was sure he heard the door close.

And when did it enter? He felt his heart hanging in space like a feather. Cold saliva started sliding down the sides of his mouth; onto his cheeks. He heard its step advance; it was so vivid. It had claws. They were angled with purpose, towards his neck. A dark masculine shadow bent over him and fangs with arrows at their points and big holes in them bent to suck his blood.

The thing sighed.

Ochieno did not hear the rest. He wanted to die.

With the pair of shorts discarded somewhere between where he stood, and the securely locked door and the shirt still in his hands, Maya sighed, again, at the head of the lover's bed. The brushing sound down the wall told him where the shirt had fallen.

Ochieno felt over-stretched like a hide in the drying yard. Like he was on punishment. Why doesn't it do it once and for all? After all you know what you have come for. Take your person! Ochieno mumbled, trembling.

As Maya made to bend and get down, something dangled from his neck and he realised that, in the hurry to catch up with the date, he had not kept away the pastor's diary that he found in clothes he had borrowed. Having discarded the pair of trousers and the shirt, he briefly fingered the diary, pondering the safest place to keep it. And then peeling off the pants with his left hand, he paused, the diary in the right hand and the pants in the left. Somehow he felt shame wearing his wife's knickers. But she belongs to me! He shrugged his right shoulder. Yes and the things of my things are my things. Full stop! And as if attempting to move ahead of his conscience, he quickly bundled the diary in the knickers and placed them next to the head of the bed.

Maya felt his urge rising, and he swallowed thick

saliva. It was warm. He was standing by the bed, his bottom at a sensuous angle. I am going to surprise you. Creep to your side, tilt your chin and slowly wake you to a warm kiss on those mango-crested lips of ours. That is the way I have chosen to begin it and that is the way you are going to have it. A baby must be left inside the place!

Ochieno had been watching this shadow in the dark, over him. He was wet. The blanket stuffed between his thighs, he was wetting himself again. His lips tried to cry but the sound remained in his throat. This time the thing itself has accompanied its footsteps. Then, he felt its warm breath. It was a male one by its odour.

Maya sank on his knees. He edged closer. But he sensed that unlike always, Tina had not applied the usual *Yolanda* perfume. He wondered. Possibly that is how she has chosen to have it. Maya tenderly lay on his side, figuring out the exact position of his lover's lips. I must sip from those mango lips. He was beginning to breathe in a funny manner.

O' my children! Ochieno bled in his heart. He was only waiting for one thing: to be touched and then after that, he would die.

Lying now very close, Maya smiled broadly in the darkness as he felt Tina's twitching eye glow in the dark. His mouth tinged and he moved his lips sensuously like a camel's before pouting them like one sipping from the *oluwo* guard.

His sight now accustomed to the darkness, Ochieno could figure out a distinct shape that seemed to focus around his throat. And then; an unmistakable breathe. His heart skipped and went numb.

Closing his eyes and fantasising the mango lips of his love, only a beat from the heart, Maya propped forward his fingers delicately like a hand picking *nakhasokhere* mushrooms.

Ochieno saw the shape of a knife now closing towards him and he mumbled some thing about who should not inherit his wives.

With the head in the forward position, Maya's hand edged forward to prop Tina's chin for a mid air kiss... and then,

A BEARD!

"O' Mama...!" His *lover* wailed

"*Lero luno!*" The *ghost* screamed.

Maya *died!*

Ochieno was wailing, shouting to the roof of his voice, calling on his clan to hurry and bear witness to this water spirit that had finally felt his throat. His more pronounced upper lip giving him the look of a squalling pig as he screamed.

Trying to grasp his whereabouts and flee is what he attempted in the next blink of an eye.

On the other side of the same room, Ochieno had collided with the *spirit* more times than the fingers and the toes on his limbs combined.

The door of the main house opened.

Maya had already unfastened that of the house in which he and Ochieno were having their circus.

"There he is!" Mirimo's rusty voice filled the night

250

air.

Tina, who had covered herself from head to toe, heard her father's words and passed out.

Outside, Mirimo aimed. Like a ploughman's whip, his spear span, rending the air, lodging in banana stems before exploding with like a corpse too long in the sun. A figure emerged from cover beneath the banana stems; Maya ran like a man sent to catch a hare with bare hands.

By the time the elder son of Mirimo helped him to uproot the spear from four banana stems it had lodged into, no dog or its barking could catch up with the most active Christian in the sub-parish.

"It was the real one. It felt my *throatiiiiii...*," Ochieno screamed with the finality of a dying man. Bundled in a corner of the room, and his voice coarse, he could not recognise the candlelight that led Mirimo and his wife in.

A shirt by the door!

A pair of trousers!

And shoes?

Mirimo paused and looked at his wife. These were the very things that the Pastor was wearing this morning when he passed as they worked in the garden. And that was shortly after their daughter had retired home, earlier than usual. He looked at Namayindi and she turned her face and looked away into the outside. Then Mirimo moved ahead and stopped, his gaze fixed to the head of the bed. Then slowly, he walked towards it until he reached it. He bent and carefully picked it. And out of it something fell. They could not believe their eyes. But as they went out of the room, Namayindi holding the hand of her cousin Ochieno, they found their elder son standing not far from where they spear was uprooted. He was peering at a bed of fresh banana leaves neatly made. Mirimo drew in a deep breath. Namayindi sighed.

*

Maya stood outside the door and called his wife. The wind blew against his back; a cold wind. The sweat on his body had suddenly disappeared; he was shivering like a reed.

"Anyango, Mama Bwire. Anyango my wife!" he whispered in hushed tone, looking over his shoulder. "Anyango, it is me, your husband Maya. Open!"

After a moment of waiting, he bent under the hem of the roof and moved to knock on the door but his hand just went through; the door was open. "Anyango, you did not close —" he said as he stepped inside. And before he could finish the sentence, his foot slid on the wet floor, spiralling him across and banging his head against the wall. The effect of this impact bounced him back in reverse, crashing his bum into the slanting pot, breaking it and spilling the remaining water. When he noticed he was not slipping any more, he remained in a squatting position for some time before rising to his feet. He realised that he must have crisscrossed the room at least twice. Then it occurred to him that in all this movement he had not made any contact with his wife. Not even the baby. His wife was not there! To be sure, he reached the door, found a support pole used for closing the door and started feeling for his wife. "Anyango,

Anyango! Are you there, mother of my child?" he did this, feeling the ground with the stick. Sensing what seemed like the bed, he bent, touched it with his hand and found only a wet mat. He went out to the mother's kitchen to get some fire to light the house.

"Mukombosi, is it you sneaking into the kitchen to steal my potatoes?"

"It is me, mother." His voice was not steady.

"What are you doing in my kitchen at this time? Don't you have a wife?" She asked harshly.

"Anyango is not there." He was poking the ashes for some embers.

"What do you mean she is not there?"

"I am telling you the house is empty, mother." His hands were now trembling and some of the embers were falling from the clay pot.

"She could be in the bush helping herself. She is a mature woman. Wherever she is, she will come back." She was not concerned.

"Did she have to go with the child?" He was now angry, approaching his hut.

"What do you mean?" she asked, putting on her *lesu* and heading for the door as Maya plucked some dry grass from the roof to fan a fire. Nakomolo came out following him into the house. By the time she reached, he had entered. The grass was damp and so it could not burn brightly. It just glowed. The house was empty. Anyango was not there. Bwire was not there. Only a strange object; coiled on the mat.

Maya approached it cautiously. The mother was

beside him. They were side by side. He first felt it with the pole carefully from a distance. When it did not uncoil, he picked it. It was a bundle securely tied in cloth. Maya's grass torch had burnt out. It was now Nakomolo providing light with her dim torch, banging it from time to time for it to come on. She moved close to light the object better. Maya untied it carefully. He opened it. They realised what it was. He counted it. It was fifteen thousand shillings. Son looked at mother and mother looked at son and none seemed to make sense of what it was.

"My son, what does this mean, son?" she was solemn.

"I do not know, mother," his voice and limbs were shaking.

"You do not know?" she paused. "And by the way, where have you been?" Nakomolo looked at her son more inquisitively, hitting the torch and lighting him closely. His head and shoulders were all soiled. "What is wrong with you, my son?" She shone her torch directly into his face and down and then her face turned away sharply. And suddenly, Maya realised he was naked.